D1024904

CHORUS

CHORUS

A Novel

Rebecca Kauffman

COUNTERPOINT
BERKELEY, CALIFORNIA

Library of Congress Cataloging-in-Publication Data
Names: Kauffman, Rebecca, author.
Title: Chorus : a novel / Rebecca Kauffman.
Description: First hardcover edition. | Berkeley, California :
    Counterpoint, 2022.
Identifiers: LCCN 2021027707 | ISBN 9781640095182
    (hardcover) | ISBN 9781640095199 (ebook)
Classification: LCC PS3611.A82325 C48 2022 | DDC 813/.6—
    dc23
LC record available at https://lccn.loc.gov/2021027707

Jacket design by Nicole Caputo
Book design by Wah-Ming Chang

COUNTERPOINT
2560 Ninth Street, Suite 318
Berkeley, CA 94710
www.counterpointpress.com

Printed in the United States of America

10 9 8 7 6 5 4 3 2 1

For A

You were born in the middle of the night

What better time for a guiding light

—BILL CALLAHAN, "Guiding Light"

The Family

Mr. and Mrs. Jim and Marie Shaw,
and their children:

Wendy

Sam

Jack

Maeve

Lane

Henry

Bette

Contents

CONTENTS

CHORUS

Proof

1929

A series of tornadoes tore eastward on May 2, 1929, touching down at locations all the way from Oklahoma to Maryland. The worst occurred in Rye Cove, Virginia, where a school building was yanked off the ground while the children were on noon recess. Desks made of oak and iron were tossed around like candy. A dumb rumor circulated about the wind sweeping feathers clean off the chickens at a neighboring farm, and hair off the cows. The terrible reality was: twelve dead children, though it took many hours of many fathers searching through debris to confirm this.

The Shaw family lived a hundred miles from Rye Cove, and well outside of the storm's path. They experienced no impact. Jim Shaw learned of the tornado and the carnage days after it occurred, from a neighbor who had listened to extensive coverage on the radio. Jim didn't discuss it with his wife nor any of his children. He carried and considered it silently as he went about his work that day, reinforcing the hog pen, training his filly for the harness, and dressing an infection near her eye. At dusk, Jim was returning the filly to her stall when his youngest son, Henry, came to him in distress. Henry was crying so hard he was drooling. The only word Jim could make out was *hanging*. Or was it *aching* or was it *ringing*?

Jim's throat felt as though it was filling with sand, and he choked, "Where?"

Henry pointed in the direction of the grove of tulip poplar trees, where the children liked to play. Jim picked him up and headed that way, running. Henry was a sensitive boy, frightened by loud sounds and long shadows and chicken bones. So it was probably merely a dead squirrel or rabbit that Henry had found, Jim thought, or that one of the other children had a bloody nose. It was probably nothing. Yet Jim's heart was whacking at his eye sockets in sheer terror as he ran with his son.

The sky was darkening overhead but still ablaze on the horizon, the sun's flames licking up over the tree line. Jim ran faster, his son's knees and elbows clamped so tight around his belly and neck that Jim could hardly find air.

When they neared the tulip poplars, Jim heard the awful thing before he saw it. He stopped running and stood still for a moment, panting. The screeching was sustained, almost with a melody. Birdlike, but only sort of. Then he saw the flapping of wings and in an instant his whole chemical composition changed, adrenaline evaporating, muscles going loose and long, his entire body sagging with the sudden lethargy of deep relief.

He set his son on the ground, said, "Wait here," and approached the scene.

An owl! A tannish thing with white and gray accents, eyes ringed with gold, ear tufts large and catlike. It shrieked as it rose and fell, lurching upward then drawn back down, tethered to the ground by some force.

When Jim drew nearer he saw fur, then the full body of a weasel that was gripping the foot of the owl in its teeth. The weasel was small, a juvenile, and each time the owl lifted off the ground in an attempt to fly away it did so with a bit of success; the weasel was partially lifted off the ground, too, its torso stretching long, but body still anchored to the ground by its hind legs. Hanging, like Henry had said.

Jim sucked in his breath and moved closer. He'd heard owls in the night and seen evidence of weasels in the morning, but had never actually laid eyes on either of these mysterious night hunters, and never could have imagined this bizarre warfare taking place before him. The owl's panic intensified with Jim's approach. It screamed and flapped harder, yet the two animals remained locked together. Jim took a few more steps forward. Behind him, Henry howled.

The weasel turned its head to glower at Jim. When it registered the size of his figure, it released its hold on the owl's foot and darted off into the dark grass. The liberated owl flew up into the dark trees. It disappeared into their shadowy boughs, then emerged above the tree line and soared in large circles. Jim was transfixed, and allowed himself to be moved by beauty; the freedom and dignity of the owl's flight filled him with such awe that for a bit he was so lost he wouldn't have known his own name.

Henry joined his father soon, placing his warm, damp hand in Jim's. He said, "I didn't want to see a dead thing."

Jim said, "I'm glad you didn't have to."

"I thought that was the only way it could possibly end," Henry said.

At supper, Henry triumphantly reported to his six siblings what he and his father had seen in the tulip poplar grove. There were no tears in his recollection.

Henry's brother Jack, who couldn't stand any excitement that didn't involve him, said, "Liar!"

His sister Maeve turned to their father and said, "Is it true?"

Jim nodded.

The children were keen to hear more details about the violence, and the outcome of the fight.

After the meal, while his sisters were cleaning up, Henry approached his father. Emboldened by his siblings' response to the story, he said, "I could tell Mommy."

Jim said, "Another time, when she's feeling better."

"Maybe the story would help her feel better," Henry offered.

Jim said again, "Another time." He tried harder to lift his

voice, but he was weary and so it was even harder than normal to impart optimism.

Mrs. Shaw was in one of her dark moods and hadn't left the bed in weeks. The older children were used to this behavior by now, but the younger ones still asked after her, still hoping for something different. Jim moved awkwardly around the topic of his wife's health, and other topics that were less complicated, too. Every single person Jim had ever encountered in his entire life mystified him, including his own children, and he often felt woefully incapable of the simplest human gestures. He worried that his efforts where his children were concerned were either wrong, or, more often, inadequate: saying too little, deferring, deflecting. He was so fearful of their faces.

Jim was relieved when Henry didn't push the idea of entering the bedroom to relay the story to his mother. Sometimes Henry didn't give up so easily.

Jim sat at the kitchen table and stared into his book of notes and numbers, as he did nearly every evening. He was tempted to ask his eldest son, Sam, to double-check his math. It wasn't that Jim was too proud to ask, he just hated to burden Sam with another task in the evening, after a hard day's work. Dared they go further into debt, Jim wondered, to purchase a gas-powered tractor? Or would it make more sense to invest in cattle? Would a healthy sow command the same price it had in years past? His mind whirred. Was the chicken coop secure enough that if either the owl or the weasel returned in the night, the eggs would be safe?

What about the rabbit hutch? So much of farming was protecting what belonged to you, and it seemed to Jim that no amount of up-keep or oversight would ever be enough in this regard; there would always be a place where the fencing was weak.

Eventually, Jim left the table to help his eldest daughter, Wendy, get the little ones ready for bed. He gave Henry extra attention, hoping the combat they had seen would not produce bad dreams.

Later in his own bed, Jim's mind meandered through pieces of his day on its way toward sleep. But when he pictured the owl and the weasel, he was already so tired, his thoughts already so detached from reality and from one another that he was certain this could not have been from his day. He had to be dreaming already, because that was not real stuff; you didn't go through life bearing witness to moments like that. And furthermore, an owl could not be real, could it? A bird with a cat-shaped head, a bird with a name like *owl* . . . ? Jim's brain skittered around, *owl, owl*, trying to find purchase with a word so strange, trying it out in different shapes, trying to believe in it.

Next to him, his wife sat up slowly and reached to her bedside table for a pill to assist her sleeping. Jim watched through one hazy half-eye. She tipped her head back to take the pill without water, and this, too, seemed almost certainly a dream—her slender neck so graceful it was impossible—until the abrupt groaning of the bed frame beneath her caused Jim to startle awake.

Heart suddenly galloping, he watched his wife settle back into bed. When her breathing slowed, Jim turned toward the window and stared out at the crust of moon that hung above the trees. He pictured the fathers of Rye Cove carrying shovels under this same moon, their streaked faces both hopeless and hopeful, digging through rubble late into the night, searching like madmen for either proof of death, or proof of life. And he knew that this beautiful world had a forked tongue. And he knew that everything he thought and felt and feared was real.

The Remembrance

1934

Maeve Shaw was pretty sure she was the only one of her siblings who was aware that it was the one-year anniversary of their mother's death. If anyone else knew, they hadn't let on. She didn't realize it herself until lunchtime, when the radio commentator announced between news segments, ". . . and one year ago today, the Washington Senators were defeated in game five of the World Series by the New York Giants, in a game that went to ten innings . . ." Mrs. Shaw's body had been discovered in the bottom of the first.

Maeve glanced around the room to see if the baseball reference sparked recognition with anyone else—it seemed it had not. Everyone was too busy talking about the mare that was about to give birth. Jack kept imitating the sounds she was making. Apparently, she'd been panting and moaning and rolling on her back all morning. Mr. Shaw and the boys had cleaned out the stall, wrapped the mare's tail, and washed her hindquarters with Pears mild soap in preparation. Now they were just waiting for the sac to break.

The boys headed back out to the barn as soon as they finished eating. Once lunch was cleaned up, Wendy, the eldest, told Maeve and her little sisters they were free to spend the afternoon as they pleased unless they had schoolwork. Maeve was very smart in school. She barely had to try, and never brought work home. Sometimes she helped her little sisters study, sometimes she didn't. Today, she was not in the mood—she was much more interested in seeing that foal get born—so she went out to the barn to join her father and brothers.

The barn smelled sweet and weird. Maeve made her way back to the mare's stall, where her father and brothers were gathered on stools, solemn and holy with expectation. It was very dark in there except for a few splinters of white sunshine, one of which rested on Henry's face. Maeve noticed in this light that Henry had an odd bruise across his forehead, perfectly centered, not a circle but a left-to-right line of faint purple, like he'd run into a table's edge, though she couldn't think of anything that would be the right height to cause this injury.

Her father offered his stool, but Maeve whispered, "I'll stand."

The mare was on her side and her dark belly, glistening with sweat, tightened with periodic contractions. Her glassy eyes rolled. Maeve eventually worked up the courage to look at her rear, and beneath her bound tail was a pinkish ruffled bulging that instantly made Maeve sick to her stomach. She closed her eyes thinking she could get over this, it was totally a normal thing, but soon realized she could not; it was not. She was on the brink of a puke.

"Yuck," she murmured, and she turned and walked away.

She heard Jack snickering behind her, but she didn't care. She was relieved when a fresh breeze reached her. It was a cool day, just cool enough for the sun to feel wonderful on her face. She didn't particularly feel like going back inside the house yet to confess to her squeamishness, so she decided to go for a walk instead. She struck out through the fields. Where the crop ended, she took the footpath into the woods, having walked far enough and fast enough that she'd gotten a little heated up and was now thinking the shade would be nice. Perhaps she'd remove her shoes and wade into the pond.

Where the path forked, she took the narrow trail leading to the pond. Red maples and laurel oaks canopied overhead.

As she neared the black water, she was startled to see that she was not alone. Just on the other side of a little outcropping of cat-tails, a young man stood with a fishing pole, his line stretched out midway across the length of the pond. He wore shabby clothing and a green derby hat. He spotted her a moment after she spotted him, and lifted his hand from the grip to wave.

Maeve knew that her father told the neighbors they were free to fish here, but Maeve also knew all the neighbor boys, and this was not one of them.

She said, "Who are you?"

"John Winthrop," he said. "Who are you?"

"I'm the landowner," she said.

"Huh?" he called, cupping a hand to his ear.

She moved closer, around the cattails. A little red tackle box was on the ground at his feet, along with half a sandwich on a piece of wax paper.

She said, "I own this pond."

"You're Jim Shaw?"

She narrowed her eyes.

He laughed. "My aunt and uncle said your father lets them fish here."

"Who's your aunt and uncle?"

"Helen and Joe."

Oh, yes, the Winthrops. "Why haven't I seen you before?" Maeve said.

"I just moved here last week. They worked it out with my parents so's I'd have room and board because my uncle Joe needed an extra hand anyway, and I wasn't able to get work around my place."

Maeve was aware that young men everywhere were still hard up for work, years after the crash. They were forever showing up at the Shaw house, asking her father for a job. Jim was always polite as he explained that he had enough help with his own sons and just couldn't afford to take on another set of hands, even at a very low wage. Sometimes they begged. Sometimes they were emaciated. It was very disheartening.

John Winthrop didn't seem disheartened, though, nor under-nourished; as a matter of fact, Maeve thought he looked rather plump for a farmhand.

She said, "Our mare is going to have a foal today."

"That right?"

She nodded. "You getting any bites?"

"Not yet." He reeled in and recast. He did so with an extra little bit of flourish, Maeve thought, like he wanted her to notice his technique.

Maeve was pretty enough to get some attention from boys, and most girls her age—fourteen—were very keen on attention from boys. But Maeve was too bossy, she couldn't hold back, and boys never seemed to stay interested in her for long.

"You want some tuna sandwich?" John Winthrop said.

"Nah." Maeve was still queasy from the mare. "Where'd you move from?"

"Chesterfield. You know where that is?"

"Yeah."

He slowly reeled in and cast again. "My aunt and uncle said your dad's a real saint."

Maeve had never heard of a person saying this about another person, unless of course they were an actual saint. She repeated, "They told you my dad's a saint?"

John Winthrop nodded.

"Why?" Maeve said.

"That's what I was going to ask you," he said. "They didn't say any more than that."

"Maybe because he lets other people fish on our pond?" Maeve suggested, though while this was a nice gesture, it didn't exactly seem worthy of sainthood.

There was of course also the way her father had cared for her mother for all those years, never raising his voice at her, never bad-mouthing her to the kids. In fact, he'd always defended his wife when one of the children—usually Maeve or Jack, who had the hardest time holding their tongues—said something nasty or demeaning about her. Mr. Shaw always said, *She can't help the way she acts sometimes. It's like a sickness. It's not who she actually* is. Did that make someone a saint, to pretend that someone who lived in a bad way could still be a good person on the inside?

Furthermore, how could Helen and Joe Winthrop possibly know any of this? They had all kept their mother's problems very private, as far as Maeve knew. At most, she thought, neighbors would have known that her mother was vaguely unwell and then that she died. It intrigued Maeve to consider that the neighbors might have known more about her mother than they let on.

She said, "You're sure they didn't say anything else about our family? For example, about my mother?"

John Winthrop shook his head. "Why? What's up with your mother?"

"She's dead," Maeve said, "for one thing."

"Oh."

They stood in silence for a bit, then John Winthrop began singing—quite badly—a tune Maeve didn't know, but she gathered it was meant to bring her some cheer. A spiritual tune, perhaps.

"I'll leave you to it," Maeve said, turning away.

He stopped singing. "I could show you how to cast," he said.

"I already know how," she said. "Ta-ta."

Mrs. Shaw had died from mistaking sleeping pills for nervousness pills. So they said. Or the other way around. And, or, well, either way, she had definitely overdone it, too. Wendy and Sam, the eldest children, had discovered their mother's dead body while the others were listening to the baseball game, and they hypothesized rather persuasively that their mother woke from a nap, and in a stupor had believed she was waking from the night's sleep, and therefore took all her strong morning doses a second time, within just a few hours of the first. Maeve could tell that Wendy and Sam badly wanted the others to believe this. Maeve wondered why they preferred that version to the other one. To Maeve's mind, a suicide would have been considerably less pathetic. Maeve understood Wendy and Sam's rationale where the youngest ones were concerned; Henry and Bette might not even know the meaning of the word *suicide*. But of course they knew their mother was not well. There were years of volatility, when you never knew what to expect. Then, eventually, you did know what to expect, because one version emerged: the pale, sorrowful, stupefied one. The last year or so of her life, she rarely left her bed and generally objected to her children entering her room, unless it was with food. Sometimes Henry and Bette fought over who got to take her a meal, that was how bad they wanted to see her. It made Maeve so mad to see how the little ones never stopped hoping. When they got in there with her food, she would rarely even look at them, much less offer a kiss. Well, anyway. No one wanted to talk about Mrs. Shaw anymore. Maeve believed this was because they were all secretly happier now and no one wanted to say so. Maeve usually assumed people felt the way she did about things. In any case, she was relieved that no mention of her mother had been made today. It seemed like the anniversary of her death would go unnoticed; there would be no remembrance.

When Maeve got back within sight of the barn, she saw that one of the boys was exiting it and heading in the direction of the house. It pleased her to imagine that she wasn't the only one who couldn't hack it in there; the pink bulge on the mare's bottom had gotten to someone else, too.

In the house, Wendy confirmed to Maeve that, yes, Henry had gotten sick over the whole ordeal and he was up in the boys' bedroom napping.

Jack came in around five to announce that the foal had been born and it basically looked like a sack of black slime. Both foal and mare were doing fine. Mr. Shaw had said not to invite anyone else to come out to see just yet, though; the mare and foal needed to relax awhile and have their first nursing and it wouldn't do to have a bunch of people in and out and staring. Mr. Shaw had also told Jack to relay that they wouldn't be in on time for supper, so the others should go ahead and eat. Henry looked like he really wanted to go back out to the barn now that his stomach was settled and the foal was born, but he didn't ask.

The girls and Henry ate and cleaned up the meal. They got out the deck of cards and played Towie around the table for a while, then Wendy dropped out because she needed to retrieve the wash from the line, so they ended the game. Maeve picked up an old magazine to read. She felt oddly worn out for a day where she hadn't done much of anything. She watched the setting sun through the window, the sky a gauzy purple, the trees becoming black skeletons. A chill advanced through the house.

Maeve went upstairs to the room she shared with her sisters to retrieve a sweater. On the way, she hesitated outside the boys' bedroom when she heard a strange rhythmic knocking sound and then a voice inside. Sam and Jack were still in the barn with their father, monitoring the foal for steady breathing and to see that it started to nurse. All the girls were still downstairs; she had just left them there moments ago. So it could only be Henry in there. And he could only be talking to himself. She pressed her ear to the door.

"I love you, Jesus," Henry's little voice was saying in a tone she'd never heard before, so odd and urgent. He spoke softly, but with force. "I love you," he insisted. "I do, Jesus."

Henry had attended a tent revival with the family of his best friend from school several weeks earlier. It wasn't the kind of thing Mr. or Mrs. Shaw had ever paid mind to. Their family only ever said grace when they had company, which was not often. They set foot in church only for weddings or funerals. None of the other children had ever been to something like a tent revival, nor had they any desire to. But Henry had really wanted to go, especially after his friend told him about the fried chicken they usually served, and the exciting speeches that were given. Mr. Shaw said he didn't see a problem with it so long as Henry was home by Sunday night. So off Henry went with his friend's family to the Appomattox fairgrounds for the weekend.

Henry had returned from the tent revival looking grave and afflicted. Jack gave him a hard time that night, saying things like, "Devil got your tongue?"

Henry hadn't said a word about the tent revival to anyone since, not that Maeve knew of anyway, and she hadn't had another thought about it until now.

Maeve peered into the keyhole, and saw that Henry was on his knees at the end of his bed, and the knocking sound was his forehead against the bed frame. She thought of the bruise she had noticed earlier that day. "I really *do* love you, Jesus," he hissed antagonistically. *Bang, bang, bang* went his little head against the wooden bar, again and again.

Maeve wanted to open the door and pull him away from the bed. She wanted to hold him tight and say, *It doesn't matter,* or, *Stop hurting yourself,* or, *It's okay if you didn't love her. I didn't, either.*

She didn't go in, though. She felt that somehow it might be worse on Henry to have his moment interrupted. Instead, she just watched, to make sure he didn't do any serious damage like knock himself out cold, and she waited for him to finish.

Maeve marveled at the prospect of how mysterious her little brother had suddenly become to her. In one instant. You knew your own life inside and out, but that was it, wasn't it? That was all you got. Every other life would contain a multitude of entanglements and obsessions and longings that you could not even imagine; every other life would remain as alien to you as if it had been lived out on the moon.

Henry kept going and going with the head knocking and the assertions of love. Eventually, Maeve grew tired of waiting for him to stop, and she was also beginning to feel some vague distress. She rapped on the door with a knuckle and entered before he had time to respond.

He scrambled to get up off the floor and stared at her with a dazed look.

She said, "It's time you stop that."

He said, "Okay."

"I mean it. I don't want you to do that anymore."

"I won't."

Maeve had no idea if he was telling the truth. She never would.

Day Trip

1951

Henry Shaw, second youngest of the Shaw siblings, was enjoying coffee on the deck of a hotel room with his wife, Anne. The early morning sea breeze was pleasant on their faces, which were stiff with sunburn. They ordered room service for breakfast when their daughter, Mimi, woke. Mimi watched her mother closely as she ate. She said, "Your hair is better than usual."

As Anne was readying her things to leave for the day, Mimi had all sorts of questions. "Are you going to talk about me to your friend? What will you say about me?" And, "Will you have trouble parking?" And, quietly, "Will I go into the men's room with Daddy, or will he come into the ladies' room with me?"

Anne was going to take the car and spend the day with a college friend who lived on Cape May, an hour away. She would return in the evening and meet Henry and Mimi at the Sunset Grill, where she had made reservations for six o'clock.

Henry spent very little one-on-one time with his daughter,

and it was clear they were all a little nervous about how it would go. He worked as an engineer with Bell Telephone Company, a job that paid well but often required overtime. Anne had her degree in elementary education and was a stay-at-home mom now but would return to teaching when Mimi started school. Sometimes Henry and Mimi played together for an hour or two so that Anne could enjoy a leisurely bath in the evening, or the odd cocktail out with a friend, but an entire day like this was very rare.

As soon as Anne was gone, Mimi spun toward her father and said, "What now, mister?"

"Beach?" Henry said.

"Boardwalk."

"All right. Let's go ahead and take our things for the beach, too, in case you want to go for a swim once we get down there." It was a fifteen-minute walk from the hotel to the waterfront.

Henry packed the canvas bag with their swimwear and Mimi's beach toys, and strapped the folding chairs onto his back. Mimi said, "Aren't you going to put sunscreen on me?" Once he had done this, she said, "Aren't you forgetting something else?"

"What's that?"

"My hat?" The yellow bucket hat fit tightly over her curls.

On the walk to the shore, Mimi grumbled about the sun in her eyes and pointed out all the hotels they passed, wondering aloud why they couldn't have stayed somewhere closer to the water.

A week at the Jersey Shore had been Anne's idea, and Henry agreed that it sounded like a fine time. The last few "vacations" the three of them had taken had been to visit Henry's father, whose health was declining, and his eldest sister, Wendy, who provided live-in care for their father, back at the family farmhouse in Virginia. These trips were not much fun for anyone, but it was important to Henry that Mimi spend some time with her grandpa Shaw before he passed. They had been to Virginia several times in the past year, though, so Henry okayed this beach trip, as long as Anne agreed to arrange the hotel and itinerary. Henry was usually up for about anything, but hated being responsible for anyone else's good time. So far it had been a great week, despite the long walk to the beach and Mimi's related grievances.

At the boardwalk, she wanted to look through the coin-operated binoculars to see if she could spot any dolphins or whales. Then they went into the store that sold hermit crabs in small wire cages. Some of the crabs had their shells painted bright colors with nail polish. Mimi had been eyeing these crabs all week, and Henry and Anne had promised they would get her one on the last day of vacation.

By now, the man who worked here knew Mimi. He said, "What's the plan for today, Miss Mimi?"

"Mommy is in Cape May with her friend," Mimi said. "So it's just me and Daddy. All day."

"I see," the man said.

"Daddy doesn't know how to take care of me," Mimi announced.

Henry and the man both laughed, and Mimi seemed disappointed that her statement had not created more drama.

Next, she wanted to watch some teenagers playing arcade games.

Now she was hot, and wanted to get in the water. Henry located a single-stall restroom separate from the public men's and women's. Once again, Mimi seemed disappointed; this time, that there had been an easy solution to the question of which of them would go into the wrong bathroom in order to change.

Down on the beach, Mimi admired a large sea turtle someone had sculpted out of sand, then gave one of his fins a kick. She picked a spot for them to settle near to the lifeguard who had given her a candy yesterday, but today the guy just waved, and Mimi muttered, "Fine, just fine."

They went to the water and Mimi reached for her father's hand. She was scared to dunk in the ocean but wanted to go in deep, so he held her, making sure to lift her up and out of the crashing waves. The sun glittered on the whitecaps. They stayed out in the water for a long time, much longer than Mimi had wanted to stay in the water any other time this week. She squealed as she clung to her father's neck, and she tossed her head back, shaking her curls. Henry felt happiness pumping through him.

Eventually, Mimi tired of this. They changed back into their clothing. It was almost noon. Anne would have been in Cape May for a few hours already.

Henry said, "What sounds good to eat?"

Mimi pointed at the fudge shop and said, "That."

"Would Mommy let you eat something sweet like that for your whole lunch?"

"What does that matter? She never asks me, *Would Daddy let you do that?*"

This all but confirmed that Anne would not allow it. "After lunch," Henry said.

"Oh, come on, just let me have it now," Mimi said, like a dare. Henry didn't really care if his daughter thought he was a wimp for caring what Mommy would do.

He wondered if Anne was eating lunch with Linda now. He pictured her sipping a glass of Chardonnay and telling Linda what her life was like these days. He pictured Anne and Linda sitting on deck chairs eating chilled shrimp, Anne in that new mint-green dress she had pressed this morning. He imagined Linda getting tipsy and asking about things in the bedroom, and he hoped Anne would say, *No complaints there!* or something like that. Henry didn't know how he stacked up against Anne's friends' husbands, in the bedroom or otherwise, but he hoped he gave her enough to be proud of. It was important to Henry that he didn't give Anne any reason to talk about him the way, for example, his younger sister, Bette, talked about her husband, Ray, yikes.

Mimi said, "Fine, then I guess I want a cheeseburger and fries."

They ate at the place with high stools lined up along a narrow stainless-steel table facing out toward the boardwalk, so that they could people-watch. Henry was pleased that Mimi picked this arrangement, which felt like considerably less pressure than sitting across from each other at an indoor table.

When Mimi had finished her fries, she lifted the paper cone they were served in to her lips and tipped it back to polish off her meal with a mouthful of salt.

Henry felt heavy-laden with fatigue when he rose from the table after the meal and asked Mimi if she wanted to head back to the room for a nap.

"What? No way!" she said. "You promised fudge."

The elderly woman behind the counter at the fudge shop was charmed by Mimi, and offered samples of every single flavor, on little squares of wax paper. After this, Mimi announced that she wanted to ride the Ferris wheel, even though earlier in the week when this activity had been suggested by Anne, Mimi had expressed reluctance. They made their way down to that end of the boardwalk, stopping at a lemonade stand because the sun was very hot now and the morning breeze had vanished altogether.

The amusement park was not busy at all this time of day; most people saved the rides for the evening when the heat was less severe. There was no line for the Ferris wheel. As they drew close, Mimi's fears seemed to resurface and when the young attendant took their tickets, she said, "Has anyone fallen?"

The young man said, "Not on my watch."

Personally, Henry was no big fan of heights either—he'd had

a bad experience as a kid—and would not have minded if Mimi opted out at the last second, but she seemed determined.

Henry asked if he could leave their beach supplies at the bottom, and the young man placed them out of the way. They boarded their carriage and the young man pressed the bar over their laps. Only a few other carriages were occupied, but with no other interested parties in sight, the young man announced through a megaphone that he would be starting shortly, then he did a countdown, then the thing groaned into action, and up they went. The carriage swayed to and fro much more than Henry would have expected, especially given that there was no discernible wind. As they approached the crest, Henry saw that Mimi's eyes were closed, her whole face screwed tightly shut.

"You okay?" he said. Mimi nodded, but then she snatched her hand from his and put it to her lips. Her whole back lurched and everything she had consumed in the last hour gushed forth from her mouth. Henry could not believe the sheer volume of what had been inside of her.

"Oh, geez," Henry said. "It's okay, honey. You're okay, Meems, don't worry."

By the time they neared the bottom of the cycle, she had stopped retching and was staring into her lap at the mess. Henry rubbed her back. He caught the young man's eye and nodded in Mimi's direction, hoping the kid would get the message. The kid pressed a few buttons and was able to bring the thing to an abrupt stop before their carriage had passed the boarding platform. He released the lock on the safety bar and stepped a comfortable distance away for them to disembark. Henry retrieved their things and mouthed, *Sorry.*

Mimi wouldn't look at the young man.

They walked a short distance so that they would be out of sight of the other Ferris wheel riders. Henry reached into the canvas bag, pulled out his damp swim trunks, and said, "Let's wipe up a little bit with these." He knelt to dab gently at her chin.

"My dress," Mimi moaned.

"We'll have a load of laundry done at the hotel," Henry said. "It will come right out."

"The smell, too?"

"Yes."

Mimi scowled. "I don't want to tell Mommy."

"Then we won't," Henry said, pleased for some reason that his daughter wanted to keep this between them. He felt like he must be doing an okay job. Then he wondered what sorts of things Mimi had asked Anne not to tell him over the years, and if Anne always obeyed.

After Henry had made arrangements for the laundry with the housekeeper, he helped Mimi with a bath, and then she was content to lie on the bed. She was asleep in no time at all. He watched her and he loved her so much. He wondered what Anne was up to now, if the ladies would shop, or spend all day at Linda's place. He wondered if Linda's rich husband was hanging around or letting the ladies have their time.

When Mimi woke, it was time to get ready for dinner. Henry showered and shaved. As he pressed his shirt, he heard Mimi playing with her doll in the other room. She spoke with a soft and soothing voice. She said, "Oh, geez, it's okay, dolly, shh-shh, don't worry." Henry moved a few feet so that he could see Mimi through the door and in the reflection of the mirror. She was stroking the doll's back gently. "It's okay, honey, it'll come right out in the wash," she said.

When Henry was dressed and ready, he helped Mimi into her blue dress and saddle shoes. He didn't know what to do about her hair, but tried his best with two barrettes. She was mellow and pleasant when they left the hotel, and Henry hoped this mood would hold until they reunited with Anne. He was feeling great about how the day had gone, but knew that any little thing on the short walk between the hotel and the restaurant could ruin that.

Anne had not yet arrived at the Sunset Grill, so the two of them went ahead and were seated in a booth next to a window. Henry looked at his watch. It was six o'clock on the dot. He had hoped that Anne might beat them there and be enjoying a cocktail at the bar, but the hostess assured him she had not checked in. Anne was usually very punctual.

The waitress came by and asked for their drink orders. Mimi got a Shirley Temple and Henry got a Coke. He barely drank alcohol anymore; couldn't hack a hangover at work, and had simply gotten out of the habit on weekends and vacation, too. There was, of course, the issue of his brother Jack, too, which made Henry extra leery of alcohol. After Jack returned from the war, he had spiraled hard. Eventually, his wife at the time, Camille, had divorced him, saying that his drinking was to blame. (Henry's eldest brother, Sam, had served, too; only Henry had missed the draft, too young by a few years.) Sam had returned from the war with his own set of issues, it seemed, but drinking was not one of them. Gross stress reaction was how their psychologist sister Maeve classified mental problems that veterans and people who had undergone other sorts of trauma, too, were likely to face: flashbacks, anxiety, hallucinations, dread, all of which could of course lead to self-medicating with alcohol. Henry shouldered guilt over having evaded the war and all these associated mental problems. In any case, after seeing what it had done to Jack, alcohol was a risk that Henry didn't want to take. He didn't judge his brother, but personally he was determined to steer clear of anything that could ever jeopardize his marriage.

He looked at his watch. It was ten minutes after now. It really was unlike Anne to be late, even just a few minutes, and especially for a nice dinner. He wondered if she was having trouble parking.

Maybe he'd go outside and watch for the car. No, he thought, silly, he couldn't leave Mimi here on her own.

When the waitress returned with a basket of bread, he said, "My wife should be here any minute."

The waitress said, "Anything else you need in the meantime?"

"I don't think so," Henry said. "Would she . . . I guess if she got here she'd check in the with the hostess right away, so she couldn't be waiting for us at the bar or something?"

"I can check," the waitress said.

"She's in a green dress, light hair," Henry said. "Actually, I'm sure she's not there, though. She made the reservation and would have checked in with the hostess. Never mind."

He buttered a roll for Mimi, who said, "Daddy, your face looks wet and wrong."

"Oh." Henry dabbed his brow with his napkin.

He ate a roll. Mimi pointed out the window and for a split second Henry thought it must be Anne arriving, but it was not, it was a child with a balloon shaped like a monkey. He looked at his watch. Nearly a quarter after six now. His whole body felt cold. Anne had *never* been this late, ever. Well, except for the one time, her friend's baby shower a year or so ago. She'd guessed she might be home from that "around two or three" on a Saturday afternoon, so naturally Henry started watching for her at one thirty. By five after three, he was in a tizzy. At ten after, he called the home where the shower was taking place, but got a busy signal. At a quarter after, he called again, still a busy signal. At three thirty he'd called the cops. The guy who answered acted like Henry was either an absolute psychopath, or a moron. "Excuse me, you said your wife is *half an hour* late?" the man said. Henry had spoken quietly into the phone so that Mimi wouldn't overhear. "She's never late, is the thing. I called the house where they're having the shower but it's a busy signal, their phone might be off the hook or something. Could you send someone to that house just to check? I have the address. I'd go myself but she's in my car for the day; hers is in the shop. So I'm home with my daughter, and I don't have a way to get there. If someone could just swing by that house to make sure my wife is okay." The guy said, "Look, sir. If you think your wife might be lying about where she is, that's a personal issue. We're not in the business of—" Henry interrupted him, "That's not it at all. She wouldn't lie, I'm just worried that something's happened—" In the middle of saying this, though, Henry glanced out the window and saw Anne turning in the drive. He breathed, "Thank Christ." He hung up the phone, splashed water on his face, and tried to settle himself in the moments before she entered. Anne was all smiles. "Sorry I'm late!" she said. "Nancy was just taking so long with the gifts. I left before she even made it halfway through. I told her I just had to get back home." Henry insisted, "It's fine! We've been having a nice time, haven't we, Meems?" He didn't dare let on how worried he'd been. He knew it was crazy, how he got sometimes.

That was the only occasion he'd ever actually called the cops, though there were other times he'd been very close.

✦ ✦ ✦

The waitress came by again to fill their water glasses, and Mimi asked for a second Shirley Temple.

Suddenly the white cloth spread over the table before them was not a cloth but a sheet, and a shape bulged beneath it. The point of a nasal bone. It was a face, Henry's mother's face, covered in a white sheet, his mother *gone*. How could this be? He'd seen his mother this morning. He'd just been listening to the baseball game with his brothers and sisters, while his mother lay in bed, just through that wall, not twenty feet from them. How had this happened? Where had she gone? How could a person just slip away from this world? How did a mother go from a mother to a pointy thing under a sheet?

Henry had made all sorts of wild attempts to understand over the years. Jesus factored heavily for a while. Dreams that felt like more. For a while, Henry could find meaning anywhere; an egg with two yolks, a stain on the ceiling. Obsessions and projections that sometimes overlapped and then fused, like drops of oil. None of it stuck, and so his little heart whirled like a top.

Well, until he met Anne, that was. He had not realized that one person could answer your life.

Henry reached forward to touch the bulge on the sheet now, which was of course not a sheet but a starchy tablecloth, and of course there was no nasal bone beneath it, not even a bulge, just a faint wrinkle. He smoothed the wrinkle with his finger, back and forth.

Mimi said, "What are you doing?"

Henry said, "What?"

When the waitress returned with Mimi's Shirley Temple, Henry cleared his throat and desperately grappled after a calm tone when he asked the waitress, "Has there been any sign of my—"

"Yes, sir, your wife just now checked in," the waitress said. "She told the hostess she ran into traffic on the way. She's just in the ladies' room now, she'll be here any moment."

"Ah," Henry said, and he felt a rush of cool relief that instantly buoyed him sky-high. He wiped his brow with his napkin. Whew, whew, he had made it through again, he would be normal by the time Anne got to the table.

Henry knew, of course, that all he'd have to do to prevent this happening again was explain himself to Anne, tell her of the panic he felt when she was late and he didn't know where she was. Anne knew the basics of what had happened with Henry's mother; she would understand. But Henry didn't want Anne to have to worry about him every time she left the house, or to behave like she was married to some paranoid, jealous lunatic; asking to use a stranger's telephone just to tell her husband she was running five minutes behind. No, Anne shouldn't have to live that way. This was his problem, not hers. Besides, Henry thought, he was going to be able to get over this on his own, because every time it happened was further proof that his paranoia was unjustified. Every time Anne came back was more evidence that she would never *not* come back.

Mimi picked the cherry out of her Shirley Temple and ate it.

"What do you think of that, Meems?" Henry said brightly, reaching for another roll. "Mommy is in the ladies' room and will be here in just a moment."

"Who cares?" Mimi said with a full, red mouth.

Henry smiled. "We had a good day together, didn't we." He laughed, even though this was true, not a joke. He couldn't help laughing, though, because there was joy in his chest and he was so light, he felt like he was about to levitate. "She'll be here in just a moment," he said a second time, and he fought the urge to keep saying it, again and again, right up until she actually appeared.

The Mouse

Jack was too good at impersonations. It made people mad, even though he was never trying to be mean, just committed to accuracy, and okay, a bit of a show-off when he knew he'd gotten one really right. Maeve's boyish stride, like she'd just dismounted a fat horse, Henry's funny way of saying certain words, Wendy's hurried manner of eating. It especially made them mad when he imitated them getting mad at him. They were all overserious, the whole lot of them. And moods were especially sour at this time of year, late February, gray days, the fun of the holidays long past, the chance of another big snow slim, spring still light-years away. Harvey the beloved orange tomcat had gotten into a fight with some other animal and now had a huge abscess on his neck. Mr. Shaw had warned the children that Harvey was likely to be infected by this abscess and die. Unemployment was still through the roof. Mr. Shaw had sold off another ten acres and was talking about needing to sell more. Germany was being an asshole. Soon,

Jack's older brother, Sam, would be old enough that if there was a call for young men to fight, he might need to go. Anyway, there were all sorts of problems, and Jack didn't appreciate the general funk around the house, so he got to thinking it was a good time for a prank to get people to lighten up a little bit.

On a Sunday morning while everyone was otherwise occupied, Jack headed out to the pond with a jar and a net, planning to snag a bullfrog and put it in the girls' bedroom. Until recently, he would have asked Maeve to join him. They used to be thick as thieves. The sibling alliances had been established early, and along natural age lines: Wendy and Sam, Jack and Maeve, and the littlest ones, Henry and Bette. This left Lane, who had unfortunately gotten stuck in the middle and was without a compatriot, being a little too mature for Henry and Bette, but not mean enough or adventuresome enough to keep up with Maeve and Jack. But lately it didn't feel like Maeve was on Jack's team. She got so pissy when he teased her nowadays, whereas she used to have a laugh. She went on long walks by herself all the time. She was not a fun person anymore.

It was cold outside and Jack instantly regretted not wearing his heavy coat, but didn't turn back for it. The wind was fiery on his cheeks. The sky was dark and overcast, though it didn't have the feel of imminent rain. The dirt path was clumped and hard beneath his feet, still partially frozen.

Jack took an indirect route to the pond, heading out to the road first instead of directly through the fields, so he could pass the bungalow that was nestled adjacent to the Shaws' soybean plot. He wanted to see how construction on the addition was coming along. After a string of reclusive homeowners who did not care to interact with neighbors and did not stay in the bungalow for very long before it went back on the market, the tiny bungalow had now been purchased by a friendly young couple who intended to double the size of the home to accommodate future children.

When he reached the bungalow, though, Jack found there was too much construction mess for him to have an opinion about what it would look like when complete. He thought of his mother, despite his best efforts; his efforts were rarely enough in this regard. When Jack was quite young, Mrs. Shaw had gone on a lot of walks, and it seemed like she often chose routes that would take her by the bungalow house, though she never lingered when there were occupants.

Jack circled back through the fields, then through the woods, where large birds shrieked at his approach, but did not lift from their perches. The dried cattails surrounding the pond were crispy with frost.

Before he got close enough to actually spot any frogs, a movement over beneath the honey locust snagged his attention. A rhythm. John Winthrop was seated against the trunk of the honey locust, his body bent but rigid in some gross need. His hand was clutched and tugging vigorously at his own lap. In Jack's startled surprise, a sound escaped him.

John Winthrop looked over sharply. The two had crossed paths a few times before; Jack knew the guy was here working for his uncle Joe, their neighbor, and up until this moment, John Winthrop was A-OK in Jack's book.

"Hey," John Winthrop hollered out in a haggard voice, straightening up and no longer tugging, but now using his hand to conceal the instrument of his activity. His green derby hat sat on the ground next to him.

Jack heard a zzzzip.

John Winthrop said, "Hey!" again, cheerier this time, like he had just solved a small problem.

Jack muttered, "God's sakes."

Of course Jack did this thing, too, but in his bathroom with the door locked, and full of shame, like a decent person. Not like this, out in the open, on another man's land for crying out loud, and for all the world to see.

John Winthrop said jovially, "Oh, come on now. Say, you wanna see something?"

Jack had already seen way too much. He felt riled up and very weird. Still, he was disinclined to just walk away like some wimp, like John Winthrop had more of a right to this spot than he did. So he said roughly, "Why don't you head on home? This isn't your land."

John Winthrop laughed. "Come on, pal," he said. He pulled something out of the hat on the ground next to him. A photograph. He waved it in the air. "You're gonna wanna see this," he said.

Jack scratched his head and gazed out over the water for a bit, then approached. He had to get within a few feet of John Winthrop, and the photograph, to see what it was. A naked woman, of course, lying on a bed facing the camera, and there was a man lying behind her and you could not see much of the man except for his arm which was cradled around her waist and his hand was over one of her breasts.

Jack looked for longer than he wanted to.

John Winthrop laughed again. He pointed down at the hat, where Jack could see that there were more pictures. "Wanna see all of them?"

Jack said, "Why don't you do this at home?"

John Winthrop shrugged one shoulder. "More fun out here."

"More fun?" This business had never seemed like fun to Jack. A necessity, a physical pleasure even, despite the shame, but that was not the same as *fun*.

John Winthrop gave him a cheeky grin. "You never know who might catch you."

Jack felt his chin jerk back into his neck. So John Winthrop *wanted* someone to show up here, to watch his display, to look at his dirty photographs with him?

John Winthrop quickly clarified, "I'm not talking about you. I'm not a homosexual." He hesitated and said, "Your sister likes looking at these photographs, you know."

Jack felt a tidal wave of blood leave his face. Maeve was the only one who ever went on walks by herself, as far as he knew.

More and more in the past few months than ever before, even on cold and unpleasant days when it didn't make any sense for a person to want to walk.

"I don't believe you," Jack said.

"It's natural," John Winthrop said. "What's the big deal?"

Jack was indignant and irate. He needed to save Maeve from the disgusting things this pig was implying about her. He spat on the ground next to John Winthrop. "You gross, fat pig."

John Winthrop scowled up at him. "If I'm so fat and gross then why does your sister—"

Jack lunged forward before John Winthrop could say another word. He grabbed him around his collar and hissed straight into his mouth, "You shut up right now, liar."

John Winthrop squirmed out of his grasp and said, "You think I'm lying, do ya?" Then he giggled. He actually giggled.

Jack wanted to rip John Winthrop's throat open. Yes, what a joke, how hilarious, that Jack's sister, his best friend, was carrying on in secret with this turd, that the two of them looked at dirty pictures together and did who-knew-what-all-else out here. *Hilarious.* Jack's whole life was such a laugh. Because how funny, too, what a laugh, that Jack's mother had been such a nutter she had offed herself, and everyone was still going around pretending it had been a mistake. What a joke! The Shaw family was just a regular old laugh factory. And here was yet another good one for you: they were poor! The farm was losing money day by day, they were selling it off acre by acre for a pittance, soon it would all be sold off and they'd be lucky if they weren't starved by the end of the year. What a riot! A real knee-slapper, Jack's life was. Laughs for days.

John Winthrop was quiet, but still giggling in his eyes. So Jack stood up, reared back, and kicked him hard in the chest, so hard that Jack lost balance and tumbled to the ground himself.

John Winthrop coughed and wheezed, and somehow found the energy to pounce while Jack was not defensive. He was on top of Jack in an instant, pinned Jack down, and pummeled him with his fists. Jack felt his brain jostle and he struggled to keep the black that was appearing in the outer corners of his eyesight from co-alescing. He felt himself stop resisting and slacken with surrender.

Satisfied that he had prevailed, John Winthrop grunted, moved off Jack, and stood above him. He kicked gently at Jack's ribs, more of a nudge, really. Jack lifted one hand meekly to give John the middle finger, in a move of crushing impotence.

Then John Winthrop and his hat and his photographs were gone.

Jack lay there for a while. His lip was busted and there was quite a lot of blood, but all his teeth felt right. He could tell one of his eyes was swollen because his peripheral vision cut off a lit-tle short. His nose was not broken, nor were any ribs as far as he could tell. *Damn him*, he thought. He'd tell his father that John Winthrop had ambushed him, attacked for no reason, like a wild animal. Jack would say he'd fought back, eventually fought that fat boy off, but that the guy was an absolute lunatic, a loose cannon. Jack would also mention, when he was sure Maeve was listening, that John Winthrop was a pervert; that in the middle of the beating, he had told Jack some really sick things, for example, what he liked to do to girls. He'd tell his father that Helen and Joe Winthrop ought to know this, and ought to be advised to keep their nephew away from the Shaw property *or else.*

By the time his house was in sight, though, Jack had lost his will to discuss any of this with anyone. He no longer felt indignant and irate, just utterly bereft, devoid of all hope. Maeve was no longer his comrade. That alliance was over. He'd gotten the tar beat out of him by a fat, trespassing perv. But tattletaling and getting John Winthrop banished from their property would just be further proof that Jack was not a man. As if he needed more of that. Instead of saying anything, Jack would simply add this incident to the collection of dark things that lived inside him; the collection that grew, and grew stronger, every day, like a muscle.

Harvey the tomcat was outside the barn, and Jack paused to give him a pet. Harvey was sitting on his haunches and scratching at the abscess on his neck with his hind paw. He scratched furiously and it was clear from the blood on his paw that he'd been at this scratching for a while.

Jack said, "Geez, stop that, you'll never heal," and he tried to interrupt the activity, gently reaching for Harvey's paw to subdue him, holding that paw back, far from the wound. Harvey was undeterred, and resumed his rabid clawing as soon as Jack had withdrawn his hand. "Suit yourself," Jack said sickly, as he turned toward the house.

The other day when Harvey had first shown up with the abscess, Mr. Shaw gave him a close examination. Bette had asked Mr. Shaw how he would have gotten a wound like that; a deep, sharp bite to the neck, but no other injuries that they could see.

Mr. Shaw said, "He's always after the mice. My best guess, he had one in his jaws and in its final moments, the mouse managed to get a good chomp."

"It bit Harvey's neck while it was hanging from his teeth, bleeding and dying?" Bette said. "Whoa." She seemed impressed.

Mr. Shaw said, "Just a guess."

Jack thought about that little mouse now, bleeding out as it hung from Harvey's jaw, knowing it was all over, knowing the end was near, but somehow mustering the energy to do some final damage on its way out. Pretty impressive damage, at that; it wasn't clear if Harvey was going to survive the infection that had resulted from the bite, and especially not if he kept scratching at it. Jack wondered if the mouse had died with its teeth sunk into the cat's neck and stayed hanging there even awhile after. He wondered if his mother had considered the fact that the final message she left for her children was that she couldn't even be bothered to write a note.

A Haunting

1952

The tingling in Bette's legs grew worse, nearly unbearable, the day Susan Peters died. Bette, the youngest of the Shaw siblings, was unaffected by news of the death, but provoked by her husband's reaction to it. Why the melodrama over some Hollywood has-been who was crazier than a bag of cats? Bette knew why, of course. Because Ray worshipped Susan Peters in *Random Harvest*, and because Ray was full of notions. He thought his notions were secrets, but Bette knew him well. Notions such as: if he'd ever met Susan Peters, she would have fallen for him and they would have married and he would have saved Susan in ways that her ex-husbands and ex-fiancés had failed to. Honest to God, Ray thought this way. He was a writer, of course.

The tingling had started months earlier in Bette's buttocks then spread south, all the way through her toes. It wasn't exactly painful. And it did not seem to be affected by how long she'd been sitting or how well she'd been sleeping or the temperature of the room, but it did seem to be exacerbated by distress. Bette had had various other inexplicable discomforts over the years, aches and itches and whatnot, but none as bothersome as this tingling. She decided she'd better see her general physician about it, and he suggested she wear warmer pants and eat more red meat. He asked if they were trying to have children and recommended that they try a little harder. Then he referred her to a neurologist, who ran some tests that came up normal. At her second appointment with the neurologist, he seemed less than thrilled to see her. He recommended massage therapy. That was several weeks ago.

Bette called the neurologist's office again the afternoon of the day that Susan Peters died, to inform him that the tingling was worse than ever, despite two massages in the past week. She left all the pertinent information with his receptionist, and said ideally she'd like to schedule an appointment to see the doctor tomorrow. The receptionist called back an hour later and told Bette that the neurologist would not be able to see her tomorrow and in fact he was actually referring her to a different doctor altogether. Furthermore, the receptionist said, the neurologist had already conferred with that doctor, and he'd managed to go ahead and get Bette an appointment set up with that doctor for tomorrow, at eight o'clock in the morning. The receptionist provided Bette with a name and address for the office, and the phone number to call should she need to cancel or change the time.

"What?" Bette said. "Who is this man now? What's his specialty?"

The receptionist said, "I don't know that, ma'am. Feel free to call that number with any questions."

Bette called the number but didn't get an answer, and decided that was okay; if the neurologist thought this was whom she ought to see, she'd take his word for it and just show up for the appointment.

Ray was still in the dumps at supper that evening, presumably still over Susan Peters, and Bette wanted to throw a plate at his head. Instead, she asked how his work had gone that day.

"Got a couple good hours in," he said.

Ray's family had loads of money on account of a timely investment in the Campbell Soup Company, so Ray's writing success (or lack thereof) mattered little. To date, the only thing he had ever published was a pretentious little short story in his college literary journal. Ray had been a writing major at Drexel University, during which time he made frequent trips up to Manhattan, to network with the who's who in publishing. His father served on boards and committees that had sway. His mother was friendly with people like Zsa Zsa Gabor. One of his fraternity brothers got a job with Simon & Schuster. So it was not for lack of opportunity or connections that Ray remained unpublished.

Even more disheartening to Bette than her husband's obvious lack of output or talent or both, was the fact that he didn't know she knew he was a fraud. It was clear he believed she was dumb.

He's waiting on feedback from an editor, she was to tell people. Or, *He just received feedback and is up to his ears in edits.* Or, *The publisher asked him to restructure his entire project, which will add, ballpark, a year to the whole process. It's going great. Early readers are comparing his work to Salinger. He's working up a storm.*

Ray was never writing when she interrupted him in his study. He was always reading a tabloid or watching television at low volume or napping upright in his chair. As far as she could tell, he hadn't written a single thing in the six years they had been married. She was pretty sure Ray had plagiarized the speech he gave at their wedding, for crying out loud.

Their wedding, to be fair to Ray and his family, was a gorgeous affair that his parents had generously financed. Bette and Ray had met in Manhattan during one of his networking trips. It was Bette's first time in Manhattan; she rode a train up to meet with a modeling agency after being scouted at a parade in Richmond. She'd have rather acted than modeled, and hoped the trip might lead to both. Instead it led to Ray. They met at a lounge where he swept her off her feet with his notions and ambitions. They were married not long after at his family's massive estate outside Philadelphia. Bette was dazzled, drunk on money and ego. She was not herself. Her father and brothers had not been able to attend, but all three of her sisters came up for the wedding and they stared around the estate like it was a museum of wonders.

Bette was twenty-five now, no longer dazzled. It was high time for children. Bette's brother Henry, whom she had always been closest to, had a daughter now whom he just adored and while this filled Bette with envy, it wasn't enough to give rise to much interest in having her own. So although she and Ray both spoke vaguely of wanting them, their efforts were lackluster. Ray's attentions were elsewhere, his fantastical notions of life with Bette had clearly faded long ago and he was developing new ones.

Ray stared grimly at his Salisbury steak and said, "I just can't believe Quine left her. That was the beginning of the end. When she really started to go downhill. The accident was one thing, then her husband up and flies the coop? Of course he'd say it wasn't about the wheelchair, but of course that's a lie. What a prick, to leave a woman in a wheelchair."

Bette said, "I read that she treated him like a dog before, and even worse after the wheelchair."

Ray shook his head with the vehemence of a small child. "Not true."

Bette chewed slowly. "I have an appointment early tomorrow morning," she said.

"For your legs?"

She nodded.

"Another massage?"

"No, a new specialist the neurologist referred me to. I gather he thinks it's quite serious. He made a call in order to get me in to see this guy right away."

"I don't think I can drive you."

"I'll drive myself."

"On account of, I'm trying to finish this new chapter," Ray said. "It's really giving me grief."

"I'll drive myself," she said again.

Ray was still asleep when she woke and readied herself early the next morning. His pink fingers were gathered below his chin like a possum playing dead. She used the atlas to determine her route and wrote down all the turns and road names. She would take the map, too, in case she got off track. It was a good distance from her home, over twenty miles, in an area she'd not been to before.

The late October air was cold and it smelled of woodsmoke. She headed south. Soon she was out of their neighborhood and into farmland with nary another soul in sight, just open road, resplendent trees of red and gold, and rolling fields. Bette felt freshness, and goodness. Her legs weren't bothering her at all at this moment. She passed through one of the little Mennonite communities, where before her a covered horse-drawn buggy ascended a large hill. She could have easily passed the thing without risking a wreck, but decided instead to slow down and follow the buggy the whole way up and over the crest. She rolled down her window to listen to the clop-clopping of the horseshoes on asphalt, and to see if she could make out conversation from within the buggy, but if there was any, it was too quiet for her to hear. When she eventually passed them, she got a glimpse of the bearded man who held the reins. It entered Bette's mind that this man's wife had probably never once had the thought that the man she married was fundamentally a weak person and a fake person.

On Bette went, and beyond the Mennonite community she was surprised to find that instead of returning to a more populous area, the directions seemed to be leading her farther and farther into rural wilderness. She passed through a long stretch of empty, undeveloped woodlands. She pulled onto the shoulder of the road to consult her directions and the map. As far as she could tell, and assuming the receptionist had given her the correct address, she was still on the proper route and only about five miles from her destination. She couldn't imagine a hospital located in nothing land like this, but maybe a large development lay just ahead.

She was still doing okay on time; it was ten to eight. She wondered if Ray was awake yet, puttering aimlessly, turning on the television to see if they were planning to run a special memorial segment honoring Susan Peters.

Bette didn't think her husband had the brass to actually divorce her. She was too essential to his image, and his image was too essential to his being. And Ray's family adored Bette. Her humble upbringing made her a novelty in their circles and bestowed them with a certain virtue. Bette didn't reckon she had the brass to actually divorce him, either. What would she do? Where would she go? Her only other home was the farmhouse she'd grown up in. Wendy, her eldest sibling, still lived there with their father. Jim had sold off nearly all his land, which was no longer making him any money. At least this way he could keep the house. His health was declining, and Wendy took care of him. Wendy was good at taking care of people. She was the type who, when troubled, instinctively reached to rub someone's back or stroke someone's hair. Their mother had been a wacko, so Wendy had basically raised all the children, and by the time Bette was grown and gone, their father was starting to need care, so Wendy had transitioned directly into this role, and never left home.

Wendy had been the one child in the family to never go to school, because their mother had deemed her too useful around the house to permit her to leave, even for an education. As far as Bette knew, her eldest sister still didn't even know how to read. (Well, maybe she'd learned as an adult. Bette did not know.) As far as Bette knew, her eldest sister had also never once gone dancing, or to a play. Bette couldn't think about Wendy, not even indirectly, without hurting. Point being, Bette couldn't go back to the Shaw family home, on account of that hurting.

A few miles up the road, the woods thinned and to Bette's relief she could plainly see a sprawling estate with buildings of different sizes, but all constructed of the same brick and in the same style. It didn't quite look like any hospital she'd ever seen; it looked more like a miniature college campus of some kind. It impressed her.

When she got right up to the driveway leading back to the complex, a sign on a stone pillar announced: REID-MILLER CENTER, and it displayed the address which, sure enough, was the one she had been provided. This was the place. It must be some kind of research center, Bette thought, one that housed all sorts of academics and practitioners. Her neurologist must think this business with her legs was truly severe. She noticed that several buildings within the complex were surrounded by tall fencing. There must be some confidential, cutting-edge research taking place here, she thought, so they needed to keep it secure.

Bette pulled in and up the driveway, which was surrounded by tall oaks. The premises were beautifully landscaped, with manicured lawns and little bulges of dark mulch lining both sides of the lane. Up ahead, Bette could see another sign posted, and when she drew close, she could tell that this one, larger than the one out front, offered a detailed directory that would surely include the name of her doctor and point her on the way.

Before she'd gotten a chance to look closely at the directory, though, movement across the lawn to her right caught her eye. She watched as a woman in a gray nightgown bolted barefoot, despite the chill, over the lawn and toward a fence. When the woman reached the fence, she grabbed it and shook it and hollered. Bette could hear the yelling but she couldn't make out the words. Then Bette noticed a man in a teal jumpsuit jogging calmly in the woman's direction. Before he reached the woman, she turned and saw him and collapsed on the ground, appearing to weep. He helped her to her feet and the two of them headed back toward the brick building from which she had come.

Bette stared, her heart ramming against her ribs.

She turned back toward the brass sign. REID-MILLER CENTER read the large print, and beneath it: *Psychiatric Hospital and Ward.*

There was a column titled *Residence Halls*, a list of identifying numbers, and corresponding arrows pointing to the right. The *Juvenile Ward* was located to the left, and *Reception/Visitation* was straight up ahead, as were *Practitioners' Offices.* This column included a list of MDs, PhDs, and LCSWs, in which Bette eventually identified the name of the doctor she was scheduled to see. He was a PsyD. Like Bette's sister Maeve. A doctor for the mentally crazy. So the neurologist had sent her here to get her head examined, possibly worse. She thought of the woman in the gray nightgown, rattling at the fence.

And she thought of her own mother, of course. In a way, Bette was always thinking of her mother. The harder she tried not to, the worse it was; sometimes it got so out of control it felt like Bette's thoughts were not her own, but were in fact her mother's, transmitted through some parallel consciousness. That was a crazy notion of course. Mrs. Shaw was long gone, and Bette had never even really known her. Everything that happened in Bette's mind was hers and hers alone.

Bette only sat with her thoughts and befuddled indignation for a few moments before deciding to get the hell out of there. No way was she going to see this doctor, or spend another second on these godforsaken grounds. But how to get out? The driveway was technically two-way but too narrow for her to just pull a U-turn.

She'd have to go all the way to the lot up ahead to turn around, where other vehicles were parked, where she would be in plain view of the people inside. Would they even let her turn around once she was there, she wondered. Or would they send out a man in a teal jumpsuit to stop her, to throw a net over her, club her skull, and drag her inside? She knew this was just her imagination, but her guts were in her throat. No, she wouldn't go any farther. She decided to just do a three-point turn here in the middle of everything, to hell with their landscaping. She'd tear through some mulch and some grass in order to do so, but it was better than going one inch closer to this place.

Zoom, zoom, zoom, Bette whipped the car around and peeled back out toward the road, half expecting to hear sirens behind her. At the entryway, instead of taking a left to return the way in which she had come, for some reason she took a right, heading farther south. She went very fast and kept an eye on the rearview mirror until Reid-Miller was fully out of sight, before slowing down.

She couldn't believe it. These men, these frauds, trying to convince her that the problem with her butt was totally in her head. She could not believe this.

Soon, Bette passed into a tranquil, long stretch of withered cornfields, the stalks bent and brown, and they moved together like a giant bedsheet in the wind. She thought of the fields that surrounded her childhood home. If she stayed on this southbound road long enough, or caught another one due south whenever this one eventually petered out, she'd get there. She had the atlas with her if she needed it. Her legs were radiant with tingling now. She was at about a quarter tank of gas.

In addition to the photographer Ray's family had hired for the wedding, a photographer from the *Tribune* was there to document the event, because of the social prominence of Ray's family. Bette was thrilled at the prospect that her image would appear in a paper with such large circulation; this was a time in her life when such things mattered a great deal to her.

Between the ceremony and reception, the *Tribune* photographer gathered and orchestrated different arrangements of family members to photograph together. *Now, the groom and his cousins. Now, the groom and his nieces and nephews. Now, the bride and her new in-laws. Now, the bride and her family.* When he realized that Bette's sisters were her only family members in attendance, he said that he would definitely want to include one of these in the bunch that would be printed.

As she posed with her sisters, Bette tried to imagine what these photos would look like in the *Tribune*. Maeve and Lane actually wore their dresses quite nicely. Both were slim, and both looked a lot like Bette, the three of them all shared their mother's delicate features. All of the Shaw children strongly resembled one or the other of their parents, versus a composite. So while the other girls looked like their mother, and one another, Wendy, on the other hand, was the spitting image of their father, with that dramatic, sharply sloped nose and dark unruly hair. And the dress Wendy wore to the wedding hung crookedly and wrong on her body, almost like a hospital gown; between that and her hair, she honestly looked a little loony. It was sad to say, but Wendy looked unfit and truly out of place anywhere but at home.

When the photographer said he was finished with that bunch, Bette called out to him brightly, weakly, "Now, how about a few with the bride and just her *middle* sisters?"

The photographer fiddled absently with his camera. "Huh?"

Bette waved her hand nervously toward Maeve and Lane. "Just me and these two? My middle sisters?" she suggested in a thin voice.

The photographer said, "Oh. All righty?"

Bette realized that what she'd hoped was not obvious was incredibly obvious. So she quickly added, "Then we'll do some with just me and my eldest sister, Wendy, too, of course. All the combinations, you know? Does that make sense?"

Wendy stepped out of the frame.

How did a person rid oneself of a memory like this, a memory with claws, a memory that never let you forget how bad you were? Bette would have happily agreed to a lobotomy if it were guaranteed to accomplish such a thing. She could not live with this memory from her wedding day. It hunted her, it haunted her, it lurked.

✦ ✦ ✦

Bette was approaching another little Mennonite community. There were no buggies on the road ahead of her but she knew it from the immaculate garden plots and the clotheslines that bowed low with the weight of their dark garments. And now, she could see a gaggle of little boys in straw hats and suspenders working together to steady a wheelbarrow piled high with brush.

At her next opportunity, Bette pulled into the driveway leading in to one of these Mennonite houses in order to turn her car around. This time, unlike at Reid-Miller, she was very careful to stay on the gravel so that she wouldn't mess up their lawn at all.

She turned around and headed back north.

The sun was fat and fiery, edging up over the tree line. A black dog dashed out suddenly from a ditch and ran, barking, after Bette's car for a while. In her rearview mirror Bette saw the very moment the dog gave up; it slowed to a trot and then stopped running altogether and sat back on its haunches, right in the middle of the road, with its tongue sagging out to one side.

In a few minutes, Bette passed the Reid-Miller Center to her left, and she forced herself to look straight ahead as she sped on by. The tingling in her legs was beginning to diminish. A flock of crows twisted up and out of a towering oak. She cracked her window open to feel a cold shock of air on her cheeks. She was going home. Only twenty miles to go now, before she'd be back where she belonged.

The Show

1933

Bette was distressed by her mother's mental condition and diminished beauty. Mrs. Shaw was spending more and more time in bed these days. When she spoke, her voice was so thin it crackled like a flame. Her skin was all wrong. Jack and Maeve seemed to feel little about their mother's decline, and they frequently made snide remarks about her, such as that she was a vampire, or a ghoul. Bette was personally offended by their insulting words but she didn't say so; Jack and Maeve scared Bette and she never liked to find herself in opposition with them. In any case, as her mother's condition worsened and the older children grew less and less interested in seeing her, Bette became more and more preoccupied with being in her mother's presence, creating all sorts of excuses to enter her bedroom. Once she was in there and had her mother's attention, Bette often clammed up, overcome by a sudden terror. She had noticed that it usually went better in there, the terror was less, if she had a planned thing to say. This was how she came up with the idea for the comedy show.

Bette toiled for a while to write three original jokes, then she shared them with Henry, closest to her in age and her best playmate, and she invited him to participate in the show. She said, "We can wear funny outfits, too. You could put the colander over your head like a hat."

They decided that the show would have three components: a schmaltzy entrance, the jokes, then a swing-dancing move they had seen at carnival shows. For this move, they would join hands, spin around a few times to get momentum, then Henry would sweep Bette off the ground, hold her out in front of his chest, and she would sing, "Ta-da!"

Last year when they did a little Christmas theater production at school, Bette had been chosen for the role of Mary, based on her ability to memorize lines and speak them clearly, and her pleasing looks. Though parents were invited, neither Mr. nor Mrs. Shaw had been able to make it. Bette still rose to the occasion, and her teacher and other mothers in attendance paid her compliments such as, *Aren't you darling!* and, *You're a natural.* This show for her mother would be a different sort of performance, being a comedy and all, but Bette was sure her talent would translate.

She and Henry practiced their routine in private, not wanting their siblings to know. Jack and Maeve would make fun. Wendy and Sam, the oldest two, would caution them against it; Wendy and Sam were always pointing out how much their mother hated deviations from an expected routine or interaction. If Lane found out about their plan she would be nice about it, Lane was always nice about everything, but there was no real need for her to know, and if she found out it was more likely that the others would, too. So when they could find time to slip away from the others, Bette and Henry practiced and worked to perfect their choreography and the delivery of each joke. Bette constructed a Raggedy Ann wig from red yarn and located red lipstick in the box of dress-up things.

Jack caught them practicing one afternoon, busting into the girls' bedroom when the two were in full costume. They froze.

Jack said, "What are you freaks doing?"

"Nothing," Henry said.

"Nothing," Bette said.

"I could hear you talking in funny voices," Jack said.

Bette said, "It's just a comedy routine."

"What for?"

"Nothing. We're just playing."

"Who are you going to do it for?"

Bette wouldn't have said so, but Henry offered, "Mom."

Jack said, "Show me."

"No," Bette said. "You'll make fun."

"I won't."

Bette and Henry exchanged a look. She thought, well, even if

Jack did make fun, maybe it would be good if they got a little practice in with an audience. And if Jack was in the right mood, maybe he would help them. In this moment, it seemed to her worth the risk.

So they did the full routine for Jack. To Bette's surprise, Jack was laughing by the end of it, and at first Bette thought surely it was a mean, mocking laughter, but his face didn't really seem that way.

Henry was panting.

Jack said, "Very funny."

Bette felt exhilaration swivel around in her. She said, "Really?"

There was a softness to Jack's face that she didn't recognize.

Jack nodded.

Henry also said, "Really?" He, too, could hardly believe Jack's reaction, could hardly trust it.

After Jack left the room, Bette and Henry shared their surprise at this affirming response.

They devised their plan for when, and how, to catch their mother at the right time, and settled on morning, after she had been served breakfast. They would ask Wendy if they could be the ones to take their mother her breakfast and retrieve her dishes. There was no guarantee that Wendy would say yes; she usually liked to assess her mother's condition before deciding if anyone other than her or Mr. Shaw ought to enter the room. If Wendy said no, they would just have to wait for another morning.

✦ ✦ ✦

The next morning, once Wendy had cleared them to take their mother her meal, Bette opened the door to the bedroom while Henry entered with the tray. Mrs. Shaw was sitting upright, back against the headboard, gazing out the window. It was warm and gray and raining lightly. Mrs. Shaw's mahogany hair looked damp around her temples. The room smelled vaguely too lived-in; all the air in there had been breathed again and again.

Henry was shaky with the tray but made it to the bed and placed it over his mother's thighs. Bette put a glass of milk on the bedside table. They hesitated while their mother looked over the breakfast, waiting to see if she would request anything else, but she gave a nod of satisfaction, and this was their cue to leave.

Henry and Bette scuttled to the bathroom, where they had placed the elements of their costumes in preparation. They quietly ran through the whole routine in there for practice. When it had been fifteen minutes since they had taken in the food, the usual wait time, they went to the bedroom door, Henry gave a knock, and they entered.

Bette was too nervous to look at her mother's face, she had to focus entirely on the performance. But Henry messed up; he looked at Mrs. Shaw. And whatever he saw made him falter, because he fumbled their entrance. He didn't do the opening jig they had planned, but just stood there.

Bette nudged him and whispered, "The first joke." It could still go off fine, she thought, the botched entrance wouldn't matter if the jokes landed.

Henry returned his full focus to Bette. He put on his stage voice and said, "Where could I find a cat with no tail?"

Bette said, "Wherever you left it!" It took everything in Bette not to look at her mother at this point, to gauge the success of this first joke. She didn't hear laughter, but she didn't hear an objection either, so she decided to press on.

"And say, Henry," Bette said. "Why are some people so tall?"

"Because their feet stink," Henry said, but he didn't deliver this line with any real gusto. His fingers trembled at his sides, like the gentle beating of wings. Bette didn't know what was wrong with her brother, but the show had to continue. So she said, even louder and more dramatically than before, "Say, Henry"—she cupped her palms around her chin—"what did the tree say to the dog?"

Henry murmured, "Nothing."

Bette stared at him. That wasn't the full line. She cleared her throat, frantically trying to animate him. She whispered, "Nothing, *what?* . . . Nothing? . . . *Why?*"

Henry said, "Nothing, because trees don't talk."

Bette couldn't wait any longer to look at her mother.

Mrs. Shaw's face was odd, like it was hanging, suspended by invisible hooks. Her eyes peered at them directly, but showed no light. Her jaw was open and a little crooked.

Bette wasn't supposed to say anything else here, the speaking parts were done, but she couldn't help herself. She didn't know what to make of this face her mother wore. Her hopes were still high. She said, "Do you get it?"

When her mother's face didn't change, Bette spoke more emphatically, as though she were addressing a toddler, or someone hard of hearing, "Do you get the jokes?"

Mrs. Shaw's jaw snapped up and she looked back and forth between the two of them and then said stiffly, "I love you."

Bette felt unbelievably deflated by this. She said, "Oh."

She could recall that when she was very tiny and her mother had not been quite so ill, her mother used to say *I love you*, some nights when she tucked them into bed.

Bette didn't know what to say. She hadn't been expecting this. She had been expecting laughter, applause, maybe a compliment. She had been expecting so much more than what they got.

Bette looked at Henry. She didn't really feel like doing the swing-dance move anymore. She didn't gather that Henry did either, so she just gave him a little nudge and gestured toward the bed. "Get the dishes," she said.

Henry retrieved the tray, and Bette waited for him at the far side of the room. She closed the door behind them a little harder and louder than she would have needed to—she wanted it to sound final—but not enough to actually make any trouble.

Back in the bathroom to change out of their costumes, Henry said, "Sorry I messed up, I got so nervous."

Bette said, "It's okay." She saw that Henry was on the brink of tears. He had always been quicker to cry than Bette, even though he was a boy, and older than her. She added, "I'm not mad at you."

Henry said, "I felt like I should say it back to her, but I didn't want to."

"I didn't either." Bette was quiet for a little bit, then she said, "I've had it with her."

She couldn't figure out why her mother couldn't just be normal and have said something like a normal mom would say, like, *What funny jokes!* or *You've got real talent.* Instead she'd said something weird, something meaningless, something that could mean anything.

Back when her mother used to say *I love you* at bedtime, Bette knew that what she really meant was, *Go to sleep*, and *Be quiet*. Because once she'd said *I love you*, that meant that she was on her way out of the room, she was gone, she was done, and she would be irritated if you called for her or bothered her again that night. Bette knew that in those instances, *I love you* meant *I'm leaving*.

Bette's thoughts were twisting and turning now, like plumes of dark smoke, and she felt sour in her belly. She thought of Jack yesterday telling them that the jokes were good. It had been unlike him to be so nice. And Bette wondered now if what Jack had meant was very different from what he said, or even the opposite. She wondered if he'd been laughing at the jokes and saying such nice things because he pitied them, and he was so sorry about their bad jokes and their pathetic attempt to get their mother's attention that he couldn't even find it in himself to be mean.

What a mess this all was. Bette felt very dark about everyone. Even sweet Henry, who was blowing his nose into a square of toilet paper now. She felt that Henry should have known better and warned her off this whole plan. Henry could be a little bit pathetic, if she was being honest. One time, years ago, Bette had overheard her brothers arguing about whether their mother loved them. Sam was saying, *I don't know.* Henry was crying and protesting, *Of course she does!* And Jack was saying, *Who cares?* Bette listened as Henry kept begging, and Sam kept refusing to answer one way or the other, and Jack kept not caring. In that moment, she had wished the other two were more like Henry. Today, though, she wished Henry would quit blowing his nose and accept the truth.

Bette pulled the yarn wig off her head and tossed it to the ground. She grabbed some toilet paper and ran it over her mouth, but it did not remove the red stain, it just smeared the color far outside her lip line so that she looked like a total mistake.

Eggshell

Henry's obsession with climbing things did not occur gradually over time, no, he simply woke up one morning with this new hook in him. He did not share his sudden compulsion with anyone, not even his little sister, Bette, whom he was closest to, because already at the very beginning he could see that it was going to put him in peril, take him to dangerous heights. He didn't want anyone else joining or trying to coax him out of it.

He quickly graduated from the popular climbing trees on the Shaw property—the sycamore from which the tire swing hung, the massive and sturdy buckeye—to other trees that had not been deemed safe for climbing. Trees that required real strategy and courage, limbs that had not been tested. Next, Henry snuck out his bedroom window and onto the roof of the house. Then he went into the attic and removed the paneled window with a screwdriver because it was not hinged. This allowed him to access the steep, narrow top tier of the roof of the house, and from there, he was even able to climb onto the chimney and enjoy that perch. Next, he used his father's ladder to access the roof of the barn. All of these endeavors Henry coordinated carefully so that he would not be caught; he could not have justified his actions to anyone.

The idea of scaling the Winthrops' feed silo reached Henry one day when he was retrieving the mail and caught a glimpse of the silo's gleaming silver dome in the distance. Henry had seen the silo up close several years earlier when the Winthrops hosted a picnic and invited all the neighbors. He could recall marveling at the height, noting its caged steel ladder and wondering if anyone actually used it, though at that time the idea of climbing the thing himself had not crossed his mind.

Henry knew his father was friendly with the Winthrops and had given them permission to fish on the Shaw pond. But he didn't imagine this gave him any right to climb their silo, so this would have to be an especially covert mission.

It was early April and the weather was cool and fresh as a root. Henry knew they were calling for a long stretch of rain starting to-morrow, so it would be best if he could get over to the silo tonight.

After supper that evening, Henry took a pair of binoculars, slipped away, and rode his bike through the fields and down the path that led to the Winthrops' property, approaching from the rear instead of from the road. He assessed the level of activity. Work seemed to have ended for the day. Lights were on in the Winthrop home. He scanned the silo up and down through his binoculars. It was an impressive structure of beveled block that was much taller than their barn. The ladder ended at a small hatch just beneath the lip of the steel dome. It would be the highest thing Henry had ever climbed, by a long shot.

He left his bike at the farthest edge of the Shaw property, and set off on foot in the direction of the silo.

The sun was halfway set, and the fields were awash with gold. Insects hissed. When Henry neared the silo, he scoped out the scene again, and was now close enough to peer into the house with his binoculars and see that Helen and Joe Winthrop and their nephew John were all in the kitchen. The ladder was located on the far side of the silo from the house, so with the family all indoors, Henry was confident his climb could go unnoticed.

The steel rungs of the ladder were sturdy and evenly spaced. They did not shift under his weight or according to the placement of his grip. He was able to scurry up quicker than he'd expected, finding an athletic pace. He wavered only once, when he glanced down between his feet and was instantly spooked at how high he was. He knew not to look. Never look. He didn't linger on this view but smashed his eyes shut to clear them, then tipped his chin up to focus on what remained of the climb.

The top rung of the ladder met the hatch, which was several feet deep and wide, easily large enough for Henry to situate himself back from the edge and enjoy the view.

Once seated on the hatch, Henry gulped in cold air, dizzy with adrenaline. He looked all around him. The curves and colors of the land were sensational. It had been a luscious spring already, the greens so intense they seemed to thump around in his eye sockets. Up here, Henry could not hear the dusk wildlife that had been actively chattering below. Up here, it was silent. No, the opposite. The wind was a roaring train. Up here, so many things seemed bizarre and useless and archaic, like language, like bodies, like the past and future, and plans. Up here, Henry could think in a big way, he tilted toward different consciousnesses. It had always puzzled Henry that everyone else seemed satisfied with this one consciousness; one familiar world, one known life, whereas Henry pined for more. Even just one more. Something that came before, or after, or ran simultaneously to this one, but on a different track. The higher in the sky Henry went, the more possible this seemed, and right now it seemed not only possible but irrefutable.

Henry drew the binoculars to his face and looked first down at the Winthrop house, then out across the land to the Benningtons' house, then to the two new homes to the east, both on plots that the Shaws used to own, one with a large barn that was still under construction, then to the new duplex near the road. Henry's father had done a lot of subdividing and selling off in the last few years. Even this Winthrop property had once been Shaw land, though it was one of the first plots to go. From what Henry understood, at one time, from this vantage point, nearly everything you could see belonged to his father. Finally, Henry looked to his house, which was too far away to make out much more than its structure, and hazy warm lights in windows.

Henry located the site of his mother's grave in the grove of tulip poplar trees west of the house. His father had made the decision to have her buried on the property because they did not belong to a church, and there was no family plot nearby.

Although Henry could not make out his mother's gravestone itself from this distance, he suddenly realized with a start that the poplars immediately surrounding her stone, located in the center of the grove, were of diminished health compared to other, neighboring trees. He never would have noticed this on the ground, but from here it was obvious that the leaves of the trees nearest her grave had a brownish hue instead of the lush green of the others. And their silhouettes were misshapen, patchy, diseased looking. What on earth? She was in a wooden coffin, Henry recalled. Was it possible that her death had leaked out of the coffin and into the ground nearby, seeping into roots, infiltrating the surrounding life?

Henry lowered the binoculars, but in doing so with a shaking hand, he momentarily lost grip of them. They were strung around his neck so would not have actually fallen to the ground, but the moment when they slipped from his fingers caused an involuntary jolt and his whole body pitched forward, his weight transferring off the safe hatch and toward the ladder and its caging. Before he knew what was happening, Henry was in a split second of free fall, and then he was hanging from the caging, gripping the thin, sharp bar painfully with both hands, legs pedaling for support. Presently, his knee met a bar on the caging and he was able to steady himself, angle onto it, and relieve the strain of his full weight so sharp on his knuckles. From there, he scooted back around to face the silo, transitioning from caging to ladder, every muscle rigid with terror.

He did not take any time there to recalibrate, but immediately started to go down the ladder.

Instinct took over on his descent. No tears, no shaking, no thinking, until he reached the bottom. There he collapsed to the ground, trembling and uttering words that meant nothing, words that felt powerful, even transformative, but that he wouldn't remember later, as though they had been spoken in tongues. He lay on the ground, so grateful for each of his bones, clutching handfuls of grass, fearful that the sky might whisk him up and away, that the sky might try to claim him.

It was dark by the time Henry made it back home. All his siblings were occupied with other things, and his absence had gone unnoticed. He felt very separate from everyone. He went to bed early.

Henry was wakened in the middle of the night by his eldest brother, Sam, shaking his shoulder. "Wake up," Sam was whispering. "Henry."

Henry blinked and looked around. Moonlight pooled across the floor. Jack was fast asleep across the room on his bunk, mouth agape.

Sam's brows were gathered. "You were having a bad dream."

"Was I?" Henry said. He couldn't remember any of it. He rarely could. Henry had a history of talking in his sleep; senseless things, apparently. And sometimes he woke to find his cheeks wet with tears. Jack did funny imitations of Henry's unintelligible midnight mumblings and whimpers. Sam was always the one to actually get up and wake Henry if it got out of hand, and Sam was always nice about this, but it still embarrassed Henry. He resented that his spirit was this way, like an eggshell, always ready to break and spill him out. Even when he was asleep!

"What was I saying?" Henry asked, rubbing his sticky eyes.

"Doesn't matter." Sam yawned. "Just a dream. Go back to sleep."

Then Henry did remember. Not what he had said in his sleep, but what he saw in it. He said, "I dreamed the world ended before it was supposed to."

Sam was already moving back to his bed, but Henry kept speaking because it felt like more than a dream. It felt like he had received something.

A while back, Henry had attended a tent revival with a friend, and returned brimming with this same feeling of conviction. It had faded with time, of course; his prayer life and interest in scripture had eventually dwindled. But now he found himself once again courting a revelation. He was in close proximity to something veritable, and he was ravenous for a truth, even a dark one.

Henry said, "The sun was gone, forever. The moon, too." He

couldn't seem to control himself. He spoke so loudly that Jack woke. "Black water came up from below, underground, to fill every crack, and it made the sound of laughing," Henry continued, as his older brothers stared at him.

Across the room, Jack said, "Henry. What are you talking about?"

Henry said, "I think it's finally all starting to make sense to me."

Jack smirked. "Congratulations."

Sam got under his covers and turned away.

Long after his older brothers had gone back to sleep, Henry's entire body still sizzled with yearning, with agony, because he was so close, so very close, to it all making sense.

Sour Milk

1926

It did not bother Sam that his younger brother Jack was more popular than him at school. In fact, Sam was grateful that his own social status was elevated by association, because Sam was too shy to seek attention or initiate friendships on his own. Boys liked Jack because he was crude, and girls liked him because he was cavalier. Sam was neither of these ways.

One day at noon when the schoolchildren went to retrieve their lunch pails, an older classmate called Jude discovered that he had forgotten to take home his milk bottle last Friday and it had been sitting there half-full beneath the coatrack, roasting in the early September heat for the entire weekend. Jude carried the bottle outside with him, to the shaded tables where the students ate lunch when the weather permitted.

"Disgusting," Jude said, taking a seat near Sam and Jack and holding the bottle up in the sunlight to examine the chunks. He offered it to Jack. "I betcha it smells worse than a pig's arsehole in July. Dare ya to give it a sniff."

Jack set his own lunch to the side, unscrewed the cap of Jude's bottle, and smelled. He let out a howl, and others farther down the table started to pay attention.

Jude laughed. He was a big, muscular kid who sported the early fur of a mustache. He and Jack palled around together quite a bit.

Sam reached into his own lunch pail and pulled out his tomato sandwich wrapped in parchment paper.

Jack hadn't yet taken an interest in his own lunch. He tipped the lip of the milk bottle. "How much'll you give me to drink the whole thing?"

"You're a sicko," Jude said. "And I don't got any money."

"How about your cookies, then?" Jack nodded toward Jude's lunch, which was spread before him and included a few dry-looking gingersnaps. Sam was surprised that Jack wanted those cookies that didn't look nearly as appetizing as the desserts their older sister, Wendy, always packed for them.

"Nah," Jude said. "I want 'em."

Jack addressed the entire table: "Who'll give me something to drink the sour milk?"

Sam felt bleak and burdened by this development. Usually Jack's antics were fun, but sometimes they stressed him out. Sam didn't want his brother to drink the milk. And it didn't seem like anyone else there was particularly keen on it either, but for some reason, Jack was determined, practically begging for an excuse to do this thing. Sam said quietly to his brother, "Just forget it. It's going to make you sick."

Jack ignored his older brother, stood up, and spoke loudly enough to ensure that all eyes were on him. "One bottle of sour milk, about to go down the hatch. Anyone wanna make bets on how long I keep it down?"

Somebody hollered, "I bet you don't make it through the whole bottle!"

Jack stepped away from the table. Dramatically, he angled the bottle back and started to guzzle the rancid milk.

Sam's own stomach lurched as he watched Jack's Adam's apple jump with the first big swallow. He no longer felt annoyance with his brother, but acute distress. Jack was going to ruin himself. Spoiled milk was like poison. Jack would throw up on the floor of the classroom before the end of the day. He'd spend the rest of the week in bed.

Fortunately, though, Jack did not make it very far. After a second swallow, he dropped the bottle to the ground, leaned forward, and retched, just as their teacher, Mrs. Tierney, was exiting the schoolhouse with her own lunch. Her eyes fixed on Jack, then she looked at the bottle on the ground, and the mess he'd spat out.

She addressed all of the students: "Everybody, back inside. You'll eat at your desks today." She turned to Jack. "What's wrong with you?"

Jack's face looked horrible, but since he had everyone's attention, he managed to give a shameless grin before wiping his white
lips on his wrist.

As the students packed their lunches back into their pails and
began to file indoors, muttering unhappily about having to eat in
the hot classroom instead of outdoors, Mrs. Tierney stopped Sam.
She pulled him aside and into the shade of the towering ash tree.

She said, "How did this happen?"

"He drank sour milk, ma'am," Sam said.

"Obviously," Mrs. Tierney said. "*Why?*"

Sam lifted a shoulder and toed the ground before him.

"I know it was Jude's milk," she said. "I heard him talking
about it indoors."

Sam nodded.

"So Jude put your brother up to it, did he?" she said. "Some
kind of a dare?"

Sam shook his head. "Not really that."

"Then why'd he do it? Did Richie and Elijah get involved?"

Richie and Elijah were the two oldest boys in school and were
known to goad the other children into doing outrageous things.

"No," Sam said.

"Then who put him up to it?" Mrs. Tierney said. "I'm going to
write up Jack for doing something gross and stupid, but I'm also
going to write up whoever else was involved. Whoever suggested
such a terrible idea should share some of the blame. Jack could've
gotten seriously sick."

Sam swallowed. "It weren't nobody else," he said, then corrected his grammar: "It wasn't anybody else. Jack wanted to do it. It was all his idea."

Mrs. Tierney absently stroked her chin with the tip of her braid. "Well, what on earth," she said. "I know your brother likes attention, but something like this? He's lucky he didn't get any more down. There is dangerous bacteria in spoiled milk. Your family farms, surely he knows the danger."

Sam nodded. "Yes, ma'am."

"So what on earth would possess him . . ." She didn't really pose this as a question, so Sam didn't feel compelled to respond.

Mrs. Tierney gazed out over the sunbaked schoolyard. Eventually, she said, "Sam, as his older brother, you should really stop him from doing things like that."

Sam was taken aback by her disapproving tone. Sam was so well-behaved, he'd never once in his life been on the receiving end of a teacher's disapproving tone, and this particular rebuke, though mild, hit a nerve. He felt like he'd been dealt a blow so hard it was impossible to tell where precisely it had landed. He froze.

The other day, one of his classmates had been talking about sleep paralysis, the sensation of being unable to move or speak or fully wake oneself, and becoming overcome by panic. Other students had quickly chimed in: *Yes, that happens to me!* and, *I've had it, too!* Sam had never experienced that phenomenon while sleeping, but had it all the time when he was awake.

"I tried, ma'am," Sam finally said shakily, although he knew that in truth he had not tried very hard. He hadn't realized it was his duty to protect his brother from his stupid self, to dispel his brother of his stupid notions and needs.

As the oldest brother, Sam was all too conscious of the fact that he lacked Wendy's intuition for fixing things, getting them right. Sam wanted to be this way, too. He wanted to be her equal when it came to looking after the others. It was not for lack of motivation or caring that he was not, but for lack of instinct and that "gut feeling" people sometimes talked about. Sam had no idea what a "gut feeling" was like. His feelings were so porous, his convictions weightless. Sam envied not only Wendy, but also the others for their sure footing. Jack, for example, even though he got it wrong all the time, he was always decisive. And little Henry, who had plenty of ideas that were wild and unwieldy, was always resolute in his thinking.

As Sam and Mrs. Tierney reentered the building, they were met by the little red-haired girl, who proudly announced, "Jack spit up in the waste bin. I sent him to the washroom and now I'm going to take him this napkin for his chin."

This little red-haired girl was totally in love with Jack and always begging him to play house with her at recess. She chased him around and said things like, *You have to hold my hand now, Jack, like a mommy and daddy, and you need to call me Mrs. Shaw,* and, *You have to pretend you've just gotten home from work, and give me a kiss.* Jack sneered at her and sometimes even said things that were downright mean like, *I wouldn't choose you if you were the last little girl on earth*, and this sort of thing just made her even crazier, made her want him even more. *I'm not a little girl!* she would shriek. *I'm your wife! Call me Mrs. Shaw!*

Mrs. Tierney told the little red-haired girl to have a seat at her desk and the girl said, "But then who's going to help Jack get himself cleaned up?"

Sam said, "I will." He knew that he was the right one for this task.

But when he actually got to the washroom and saw Jack bent crookedly over a toilet and spitting, he was no longer sure. Inside Sam, something turned, it was suddenly and unexpectedly winter, and there was nothing he could do but shiver and wait for it to pass and see what came next.

Escape

1932

Something about his boys' voices immediately struck Jim as wrong. Or at least, off. Then he thought, no, just different, though he couldn't say exactly how, or why. Henry was whining quietly about a half-picked-off scab and Sam and Jack were remarking about the heat and their thirst as they set up stools and pails, and situated themselves next to the milking cows.

Jim was in the loft, directly above them. So he could hear his sons clearly and see fragments of the scene below through rotted knots in the deteriorating floorboards and narrow splits between them, but the boys were unaware of him. The loft was not put to much use these days—Jim was only up there because he was looking for the valve spring compressor that had gone missing—so the boys would have had no reason to believe their father was within earshot. The air up there felt dense with invisible filth. Jim was bent over a small pile of rusted bolts and scrap metal and other debris, and his shirt clung to his sticky back. Acting on what felt more like instinct than a conscious attempt to eavesdrop, Jim paused his search upon their entry, grew very still, and trained his ears on what was happening below. Dusty sunlight swirled before his eyes. Soon, he could hear the rhythmic ping of milk hitting the aluminum pails.

Henry, who had allergies, sneezed a few times, then said, "You were gonna tell us about what's buried?"

"Oh, right," Jack said. "Where was I?"

Voice thick with mucus, Henry said, "The beginning. This is just one of your made-up stories, right?"

Jack said, "All this land was hog farm once, before our family bought it. Every direction as far as you can see, just pigs and their shit. Hundreds of 'em. Maybe even a thousand. One day, the farmer who lived here accidentally put cement powder in the hogs' feed."

"What! Nuh-uh," Henry said.

The Jersey that Sam was milking brayed and took a step. Sam slapped her, and adjusted the placement of his pail.

"Those hogs ate up all the cement powder in their food," Jack said, "and in their bellies, it mixed with their stomach juices and solidified to concrete."

Sam chuckled.

Jack said, "So those hogs died the next day, weighing three times more than they did when they were alive. Well, they were too heavy to move, not even five men could lift one of them, so they just had to bury them right there where they were. Dug a huge hole right next to each pig and rolled them in."

Now Sam was really laughing.

Henry was hyperventilating in anticipation of a sneeze. He heaved, "Gross!"

Jim had heard this tall tale of pigs and concrete when he was a boy, and was amazed that it was still circulating. He wiped his brow with the back of his wrist and adjusted his posture gingerly to avoid cracking a knee, or a shift of his weight that might produce noise from the floorboard.

On the ground floor, it was quiet for a bit. Sam got up, twisted, and released a moan, and sat back down. He adjusted the gauze filter over his pail.

Jack asked him if his back was feeling better.

"Better than last week," Sam said, "but I bungled it again yesterday chopping wood."

An unpleasantness prickled through Jim. Not only was he unaware that Sam had hurt his back last week, but he had also been chopping wood with Sam yesterday, when Sam had supposedly re-injured it. Now, Jim recalled a moment when Sam had winced and stepped away from the block. Jim had not asked Sam if he was okay; he'd assumed it was just the heat and that Sam would work through it, which Sam had. But the initial injury was obviously bad enough that Sam had either mentioned it to his brothers, or one of them had noticed him nursing it—which Jim had not—and inquired.

"Oh, no." Henry's voice broke the silence. "There's that rat with the fur burned off his belly."

Jack said, "Where?"

"It ran across that wall and went out through that hole again." Henry pointed.

Jack left his milking station to check out the rat's hole, disappearing for a bit while his brothers milked in silence. The pause in conversation gave Jim time to consider his first observation, that the boys sounded different from this vantage point. Was it simply the acoustics in here, creating distortions? Each of them had a slightly unusual cadence to their speech, something that struck Jim as slightly false. Close to themselves, but not quite the version he was used to. Jim fanned himself. His face was slick with sweat and he was itching all over. Like Henry, he had sneezes brewing.

Jack returned, and the boys started chattering again. Henry was still seeking confirmation that the pig story was made up.

"What *was* this land before us?" he wondered.

Sam said, "It has something to do with Mom's family, I think, even though they weren't farmers. And maybe it's got something to do with the bungalow. Can't remember."

Jim's wife discouraged talk of the history of the land and the bungalow that sat in close proximity to their fields, because she found it a painful reminder of severed ties in her family. So Jim had always been vague in his retelling of the Shaws' acquisition of the property. Before he could linger on this, though, Jim startled when a new voice entered the mix. It was so loud and so unexpected that for a moment it seemed as though it had materialized there in the loft with him. It had not; it was merely that

Maeve's voice, high-pitched and authoritative, carried differently than her brothers', and she had appeared in the doorway directly below Jim.

Maeve announced, "I could kill all three of you."

Henry responded tremulously, "Why?"

"Not why, *how*," Maeve said.

Jim peered between the floorboards to watch as Maeve unveiled a fistful of weeds.

Henry said, "What is it?"

"Jimsonweed," she said. "Thorn apple. If I dried it up and ground it into a powder and put it in your supper you'd drop dead."

Jack said, "Big whoop."

Henry said, "Where'd you find it?"

"Out in the east pasture. It was in one of those pictures we talked about in school. Weren't you guys listening?"

Jack said, "It's just an old weed. Those things are everywhere."

"If it's just an old weed," Maeve challenged him, "then why don't you eat it right now?"

Jim watched as Maeve strode back over to Jack's milking station and thrust her fist in his face.

Jack swatted her hand away. "Not after it's been sweated on by your gross little fingers."

Sam snickered.

Maeve turned and marched out of the barn without another word. When she was gone, Sam said, "She's weird these days."

Henry said, "It's because that boy with the rotted-looking

lip we keep seeing at the cattle auctions used to like her but he stopped because she's too terrible."

Sam said, "Oh, that's right."

Jack said, "Nah, Maeve doesn't care about that kind of stuff."

Jim's head spun. Maeve liked a boy with a rotted lip—whatever that meant—from the cattle auctions? And all three of her brothers knew, and held opinions about it?

Sam said, "I don't know what she expects, mouthing off the way she does."

Henry said woefully, "I don't think she can help her mouth."

Their voices got a little quieter. Jim craned his neck but could not quite make out what they were saying. Then, abruptly, he stiffened. If they were talking openly about Maeve now that they knew she was not within earshot, eventually they would start talking about their other sisters. And then surely, inevitably, they would move on to their parents. Jim understood the present danger, as it teetered closer and closer to his ears. Jim always stopped the children from speaking ill of their mother, but of course he had no idea what they said about her when he was not around to defend her; nor did he have any idea what they said about him. He marveled at the fact that he had never even wondered about this, because now, the idea of hearing his sons' uncensored opinions filled him with such dread that his mind raced toward ways to end the conversation below, or change its course, without revealing himself.

When their voices became audible again, Jim realized that the trajectory of their conversation had accelerated even faster than he had imagined, because now Jack was saying spitefully: ". . . not like she'll get out of bed anytime soon."

Jim knew it could only be their mother that Jack was talking about, in that particular tone of voice, and with that particular accusation. Whatever was going to be said, they were hurtling toward it. Jim tried to prepare himself. He tried to feel strong about himself and his life.

Henry said timidly, "Maybe she will get better soon."

No, no! Jim thought fiercely. *Don't say that*, he thought, *Don't hope*. He was certain that any words of support or in defense of her would only amplify the brutality of the reaction from Sam or Jack.

But miraculously, the conversation ended right there; neither Jack nor Sam responded. Jim couldn't believe it. Was someone's pail full and they had gone to transfer it to the cooling tank? He stared down. No one had moved. Had Sam and Jack not heard the last thing Henry had said? No, it was not possible that they had both missed it when Jim had heard it so clearly. Were they both just contemplating their retort, and the cruel thing was still coming?

But another minute passed, and nothing more was said; Henry's words were the last ones spoken on the matter; Henry's hope was still lingering in the hot air all around them.

When Jack next spoke, it was to ask Sam if he wanted help moving his pail, with the sore back and all. Sam said yes. Jim had never heard Jack offer to help Sam, but based on the natural manner of Sam's response, he gathered it was a normal thing. Did the boys only offer help to one another when Jim wasn't around? Or maybe they helped one another all the time, and Jim had simply failed to notice. He couldn't seem to get straight in his mind who his sons actually were.

In any case, if Sam's pail was full that meant the Jersey cow was almost empty, and they would all be finished milking soon. All three pails would be dumped in the cooling tank and all three boys would leave the barn to go rinse the pails and their hands, and Jim would be able to come down from the loft undetected. He would be spared.

But he knew now that his heart had limits; lines that could not be crossed. And he felt relief, and gratitude, and pride, and love, and fear, at the people his children were—both when they knew their father was listening and when they didn't—and the people they were becoming, and the things they said, and the things they didn't.

The Curtain

1936

Everything was decided by the Winthrop family: John would marry Lane Shaw right away, though there would not be a ceremony or celebration. It would be a simple, private courthouse affair. Then the newlyweds would move down to Chesterfield and into the home of John's parents, whose financial circumstances had rebounded in recent years. Joe and Helen Winthrop would replace their nephew with a proper hired hand. In Chesterfield, John would work alongside his father at the paper mill and Mrs. Winthrop would help Lane with the baby. It was all settled, the Winthrops said, it was going to work out just dandy.

Lane's siblings were deeply unhappy with this arrangement. Once they had adjusted to the shocking news of their sister's pregnancy, they quickly became enthused about having a baby around, but were far less enthused about the prospect of having John Winthrop around. Several of them, especially Jack, were vehement, and implored Lane to reject the Winthrops' proposal, arguing that the baby should be raised a Shaw, that there would be plenty of help around their house and there was no need for Lane to marry so young, nor to acknowledge the baby's father at all. Jack did not have nice things to say about John Winthrop. But John Winthrop kept showing up at their home with all sorts of gifts and promises and favorable photographs of Chesterfield, and his parents wrote letters, one after another, to both Lane and her father, to plead their case.

Jim said the decision was ultimately up to Lane. Lane didn't know how to make everyone happy. Eventually she was worn down by the persistence of the Winthrops, who seemed like they would not respond gracefully to a rejection.

Mr. and Mrs. Winthrop had a room all set up for John, Lane, and the baby by the time they made it down to Chesterfield. Mr. Winthrop had built a crib, and Mrs. Winthrop had crocheted blankets and little hats. Mr. and Mrs. Winthrop were very different in person than they had been in their letters. Now that they had gotten their way, they were not pushy at all.

John strongly resembled his mother. Mrs. Winthrop was plump and pink and had a broad, toothy smile. She drew in her breath and said to Lane, "My, you're . . . a *pretty* thing," and it seemed like there was something else relating to Lane's appearance that she wanted to comment on, but she restrained herself. She admired the wedding bands the two wore, and she touched

Lane's belly. Lane was seven months along and showing plenty, though still very lean everywhere else. Mr. and Mrs. Winthrop helped with their bags and getting settled and told the young couple that they should make themselves at home and feel free to nap before supper.

The room was bright and warm and Lane was tired, so she slept while John unpacked their things and made a few minor adjustments to the layout of the room.

Supper was very rich, both the meat and the vegetables served with creamy sauce, and there was cake for dessert. After eating, Lane helped Mrs. Winthrop with the dishes while the men drank beer in the living room. Mrs. Winthrop made friendly small talk, asking Lane many questions about her family and home. She said, "And John says you love to read."

Lane nodded. Books had been her best companions for a long time. Since all of her siblings were paired up except for her (Wendy and Sam, Jack and Maeve, and Henry and Bette), as the odd one out, Lane had been at her happiest when immersed in faraway, fantastical worlds of her own.

Mrs. Winthrop said, "We'll go to the library in town tomorrow, just you and me, and you can pick out anything you want. How does that sound?"

Lane said, "I'd love that."

"And we can do any shopping in town you want, too. Are there other things you'd like to look for? Clothing, or anything for your room? We want you to be very comfortable here."

"Not that I can think of, thank you."

Mrs. Winthrop tapped her chin with her finger. "Oh, *I* know, I'll take you to Jeb's. He's a chocolatier. You're so slim. We'll get you a whole box of chocolates, he lets you pick your arrangement, every single piece, and he always has samples out, too. Do you like chocolate?"

Lane nodded. "Thank you."

"And then," Mrs. Winthrop said, "I'll take you to MayField's for lunch. Pastrami sandwiches. It's a nice part of town to just walk around in, too. Only if you have the energy, of course." She gazed at Lane with some mix of hope and desperation.

"Yes," Lane said. She didn't know what else to say.

Mrs. Winthrop clapped her hands together. "Okay. Let's get you to bed then, shall we? You must be tuckered out from the travel. Or would you like a warm bath? I could get one started."

"I think I'll just turn in," Lane said.

Mrs. Winthrop called into the living room, "John? Come give your wife a kiss good night. She's going to turn in."

John came to the kitchen smelling of beer, and Mrs. Winthrop watched as her son kissed Lane's cheek and then he kissed her belly, through her dress. He did this a lot nowadays.

When he came to bed an hour or two later, Lane pretended she was already asleep. Even though it had been over a month since they were legally married in the courthouse, they hadn't yet spent a night together. Lane hadn't felt comfortable staying at Joe and Helen's, even though they had offered once the marriage was finalized. And in the Shaw house, certain members of Lane's family had made it clear John was not welcome to spend the night there—not that Lane would have particularly wanted that, either.

Lane had not been looking forward to sharing a bed with John, mostly because she didn't know what to expect (she didn't know what was expected of her) and she was too shy to bring it up with him. It seemed, though, that he'd drunk enough beer with his father to be quite worn out. He undressed except for his underpants and fell asleep almost immediately.

The next day, John and his father left for the paper mill at eight in the morning. Lane and Mrs. Winthrop cleaned up breakfast, then went on their outing. Lane picked out many books at the library and would have been happy to spend the whole day there. They got two boxes of chocolates from Jeb. Mrs. Winthrop drank a glass of cordial with lunch, then a second one, as they sat outdoors in the shade.

When she had finished the second glass of cordial, Mrs. Winthrop placed her hand over Lane's on the table and leaned in close. Her breath was sweet. She said, "Even though you're married now, you don't need to be . . . *wifely*, in a way. Do you know what I mean, dear? In the bedroom way, I mean. Not when you're with child."

Lane said, "Okay." Mrs. Winthrop's palm lay damp and heavy over her knuckles.

Mrs. Winthrop added, "And for a good while after, too. You'll be very sore for quite some time."

Lane was blushing.

"John will understand," Mrs. Winthrop said. "I could tell him if you want me to, or his father could, just so he knows what's right to expect."

"Okay," Lane said, not wanting to ask directly, but hoping that Mr. or Mrs. Winthrop would have this conversation with John.

Mrs. Winthrop nodded as though she had received the message.

Lane was tired by now, and Mrs. Winthrop said she would enjoy a nap, too, so they went home instead of walking or shopping more. When Lane woke from her nap, she read until it was time to start on supper. The men came home and they all ate together, then soon enough it was time for bed. Tonight, John did not stay up drinking beer with his father, but came to bed with Lane. He stroked her hair and told her how happy he was for their life together and she said that she was, too.

On Lane's next outing with Mrs. Winthrop, Mrs. Winthrop brought up Lane's mother after two cordials. "John said she passed. I'm so sorry, dear. Was she ill?"

Lane nodded.

Lane's mother's death was hard for Lane to remember even though it had only been a few years ago. The children had all been listening to a baseball game, that much she could recall. Otherwise, that whole day was hazy and indistinct in Lane's head, even including the part where she saw her mother's deceased body. So odd that she couldn't remember that. You'd think a person would never forget their mother's dead face. But every time Lane got close to a memory of it, it was like a curtain dropped in her brain, swoosh, and everything just went dark. Mrs. Shaw had taken too many of her pills, but nobody knew exactly how or why. There had been fights about this aspect, over the years. Wendy and Sam, who had found her, insisted that it had been a mistake, and Henry and Bette accepted this version. Jack and Maeve were convinced it was on purpose. Lane couldn't decide whose side she was on and so she didn't offer an opinion. Mr. Shaw didn't seem to appreciate talk of it, one way or another.

Mrs. Winthrop said, "I hope one day you'll see me as a mother."

Lane said, "Okay."

They walked just a few blocks together before heading home for the afternoon.

The ensuing days followed this same pattern: breakfast with the men, into town for the library, shopping, lunch and cordial, and some awkward line of questioning from a slightly drunk Mrs. Winthrop, then home to rest for a few hours before it was time to cook supper.

One afternoon, after three glasses of cordial instead of her usual two, Mrs. Winthrop said, "I hope you won't take this personal. It's just, you're so slim. How old are you, my dear?"

Lane was a little taken aback; surely John had told his parents her age. "Fifteen."

"Okay." Mrs. Winthrop drew an index finger across her damp brow, like she was relieved.

Lane gazed at her. "Did John tell you different?" Ordinarily she wouldn't be so audacious with a question.

Mrs. Winthrop sipped her cordial. "No," she said. "I just forgot."

Lane tried to put this out of her mind but found herself unable, so she brought it up with John that night in bed. She said, "Your mother asked me my age today."

He brushed a little hair away from Lane's face. "What did you say?"

"Well, I told her fifteen, of course. Did you tell her something different?"

"Before we moved down," he said, with some difficulty, "I exaggerated a little bit. Laney . . ." A pained look passed over his face. "You know how people judge sometimes. Like your family did."

Yes, her family had judged, about the age. She was fifteen. He was twenty. It was not a crazy difference at all, plenty of couples had a larger spread between them. Still, her family had harped on this for a while, and bombarded her with questions that they seemed to feel were closely related to the age issue, and entirely relevant. *Did he force you?* her father and brothers demanded. Jack had been particularly vigorous with his questioning. And her sisters asked: *Did you want to?* And they all said, *Tell the truth, Lane.* They all insisted in the gravest tones: *Lane, you must tell us the truth.* Time and time again, Lane answered these questions the same way: no, he had not forced her, and yes, she had wanted to. She answered this way because honestly she could not remember the moment well enough to answer in a way that might possibly get John into trouble. Truly, all she could remember were the moments leading up to it; how badly he had wanted to. Lane hated to see a person so badly wanting.

"They were just being protective," she said to him now. "We've been over this."

"I was worried about getting flak from my parents about it, too. My mom brought it up after you went to bed the first night down here. She said you looked awful young, and I told her, yes, you were a little younger than I'd first let on. But also how you do look really young for your age. And I explained how it was all right and squared away with your family, and with the courts. So she dropped it then. I don't know why she brought it up with you."

Lane said, "Okay." She thought, of course Mrs. Winthrop did not want to have a bad man for a son any more than Lane wanted one for a husband. It seemed it was going to be up to Lane to offer reassurances on this point, to everyone involved.

John went to sleep quickly, and Lane lay awake for a while, thinking about some things. Had she been wrong to work so hard to convince her family of things she herself was unconvinced of? She tried for the thousandth time to remember. It had started with half a sandwich, when she was out reading in the shade of a tree, and he had shown up to fish. The next time after that, he taught her how to cast, with his big hands over her small ones. He sang cheery tunes. Then there was a kiss. Then there were the pictures he showed her, and some gentle touching, some imitating of what they saw in the photos, though always over their clothing. All of this Lane remembered clearly, and all of this was exciting, it made her feel grown-up. It was a real version of the sort of love she read about in her books.

But then there was the actual thing that had happened, which, no matter how hard Lane tried to pin down the memory in her mind, like her mother's dead face, it was still just a blur of confusion, except for his pathetic wanting that preceded it. But everything else that had happened before the actual thing, and everything that had happened since—every word that had passed between them, every moment spent in each other's presence—in all of this, John had been gentle and kind. So why should she assume that what had happened in that actual moment was not? Truly, she had no evidence to suggest that that moment was any different than any other. That was why she had gone to great lengths to protect his reputation with her family; because she had no hard proof that he deserved less, and you could not hold something against a person that you couldn't even really remember.

Lane went into labor several weeks early. Even though most women gave birth at home, Mrs. Winthrop was adamant they get to the hospital on account of Lane's size—she just couldn't imagine a full-sized baby coming out of such a tiny girl.

They got Lane to the hospital on time, and after a few hours of painful and unproductive labor, she was given morphine and a light anesthetic. This was meant to help her relax, possibly even sleep, but the pain was far too severe. When Mr. and Mrs. Winthrop were not in the room, Lane asked John to ask his parents to leave but in a nice way, and he did, so then it was just the two of them.

She spent two more full days and nights laboring, writhing in terrible pain. The hospital staff came and went during shift changes. John only left her side to use the restroom or to retrieve food. He let her squeeze and claw madly at his arm, he wept when she wept, then he smoothed her hair and spoke encouraging words to her. He watched her with love and fear in his eyes.

Eventually, the doctor decided to go ahead with the episiotomy, or, cutting her opening to be bigger so that the baby could fit out. They explained it in different terms, of course, but Lane got the message. They upped her anesthetic and told her to just lie back and close her eyes. John nearly passed out from the blood, but even when they told him he really ought to leave the room, he refused. Lane was terrified. Everything felt so wild. They pulled the baby out with forceps. He was not breathing properly, so they immediately took him to a different room, before Lane got to hold him. Instead of going with the child, John stayed in Lane's room as the doctor stitched her up.

Late that night, little Thomas Winthrop's breathing stabilized and a nurse brought him into Lane's room. John happened to be in the restroom at the moment, and so Lane had a full minute alone in the room with her son, before her husband returned.

The moon shone bright and blue through the window. When the full weight of her child's head was against her chest, his flesh on her flesh, Lane felt everything inside her drop. What she felt in this moment was simpler and more straightforward than anything she could recall feeling ever before in her life; it was a pure explosion of emotion, crystal clear as glass. So immediate, so unadulterated, so profound, Lane thought, it was almost like she, too, had just been born; so stark was the distinction between the before and the after. And in one instant, Lane understood that there was nothing she would not do for this child. Even as she felt the throb of pain in her pelvis and the protuberance and itching of all eighteen stitches, she looked at the baby with the purest love, everything was right, and she thought, *I would do it again and again for you. Anything.* There was nothing Lane would not endure. For this child, she would willingly, gladly even, lie back, close her eyes, and allow her body to be ripped in half once again, right up the middle, like it was nothing.

One or Two Nights

1950

Jack called Maeve after the fight with his wife. It was noon and he was sober. The fight was about last night, of course; Jack didn't remember a thing about last night, and knowing that he wouldn't, Camille had decided to save up the fight for the light of a fresh day. She told him they'd left the barbecue early because he'd passed out at the dinner table, right into the ketchup on his plate. She told him that once they were home, he'd knocked two bottles of beer off the counter. She pointed out all the broken glass in the trash. She told him that he'd pissed himself on the couch, and there was evidence of this, too. Then she told him she was filing for divorce unless he got himself cleaned up. Oh, and her cousin was still planning to come for a visit tonight and God help them all if the couch hadn't dried out by the time her cousin arrived.

Jack didn't put up much of a stink. He believed everything Camille said about how he'd behaved. He told her he would spend the rest of the weekend at his sister Maeve's house, so Camille and her cousin could have a nice time without Camille having to worry about him, and he promised that when he came home he would start AA meetings again. Jack always went to Maeve's when there was trouble, and also sometimes just for fun.

Then Jack called Maeve and asked about spending the weekend, either one or two nights. He didn't tell her about the fight. He just said Camille had plans for the weekend, and he thought it would be nice to come spend a little time in the city.

Maeve said, "Goody, I'll try and finish all my grading this afternoon. What time should I expect you?"

Jack said he'd aim for four.

Maeve had a six-pack chilling when he got there. They took the beer and a box of crackers out onto the little deck of her apartment, overlooking student housing in the Norwood neighborhood of Cincinnati. Maeve had moved there some time ago to get her degree, and was currently fulfilling research and teaching requirements. Jack had moved there a few years ago, after returning from service, to be close to Maeve, and to get a degree himself. He actually moved in to Maeve's apartment and slept on her couch for several months until he found a place of his own. They had gotten on well as roommates. School hadn't suited Jack, though, and he dropped out after a semester, but not before meeting Camille in one of his classes. The two of them started dating, then eventually married and moved up to Hamilton. These days, Jack worked at a manufacturing plant and he only made it into the city to see Maeve for infrequent visits. Maeve, whose apartment was walking distance from campus, did not have a car so she never came out to spend time at Jack and Camille's home.

Jack lit a cigarette and sipped his beer, feeling restored. "How was your week?"

"My students are so dull. Lazy minds. They have no opinions, not even on really interesting stuff. Clark Hull, *Principles of Behavior*, for example. Animal-based learning."

Jack nodded like he knew what she was talking about. He'd never quite gotten over the fact of how much smarter his little sister was than him. He wondered if her lazy-minded students were smarter than him. Probably so.

Three stories down, on the street, a shiny black Tucker Torpedo idled in front of another apartment building and Jack whistled in admiration at the car, and then at the girls who came out of the building when the driver tooted his horn.

He said, "You have summer plans?"

"I should get home to see Wendy and Dad at some point. Can I borrow your car? Or better yet, we could go together."

"Sure thing," Jack said. He and Maeve had had this conversation a number of times before, but the trip home to Virginia had yet to materialize.

"Have you talked to Sam lately?" Maeve said.

Jack shook his head. "You know how I am about phone calls."

"I haven't either. I wonder how he likes running the cannery these days."

"I'm sure Rose hasn't given him the opportunity to decide how he likes it." Jack made a talking puppet of his hand and spoke in a clippy Northeastern accent: "Sam is happy as a clam. Sam is loving every minute. Sam is in paradise every single moment of every single day."

Maeve laughed. "Some people like being told how they feel," she said. "None of our business, is it?" She finished her beer and opened another one. "What do you want for dinner?"

"I like that fish and chips place," Jack said.

"Oh gawd, that place is a zoo on a Friday night."

"Please?" A zoo was precisely what Jack had in mind for tonight.

"Okay. Let's get the pullout made up for you first so we don't have to fuss with it when we get back."

The tables were all full, so they ate at the bar, which was thick with smoke and the smell of sweat and fish grease. Maeve waved across the way to one of her colleagues.

Jack said, "I'm too stuffed to split a pitcher. Whiskey for the next round?"

Maeve ate a fry. "Why not."

"That's a sport. See, you never come down on me about having a drink."

Maeve lowered her chin. "Did Camille kick you out again? Is that why you're here?"

"Sort of. No, she didn't kick me out, we just had a fight. But I'm not out of control, am I? Running amok? I'm no animal. I just like to have a drink and a laugh, don't I? I don't know why she thinks I'm such a disgrace, can't bear to be in my presence when I'm drinking. You seem to be managing just fine."

"She's your wife. I'm your sister. It's different, what we're expected to tolerate."

"Why?"

"For starters, Camille chose you. I didn't."

"Huh?"

"We came into this world bound together, you and me, whereas she chose to marry you based on information she had at the time. Are you drinking more now than you did before you were married?"

"Maybe."

"So she might feel like her choice to marry you was made on false pretenses."

Jack sniffed. "I married her because she was nice to me before we were married, turns out that was a false pretense, too."

Maeve laughed.

Jack hadn't only married Camille because she was once nice to him. Camille was a total catch, and Jack loved her very much. He just wished she'd lay off with the drama and divorce threats.

Jack said, "Say, it's our old mum's birthday, isn't it?"

Maeve tipped back her head. "You're right, how about that. Do you think of it every single year?"

Jack nodded. "Even when I was serving. Something in my head always goes there, won't ever let the day just pass by. Not like I think on it long or hard, though. And not like I've got anything nice to say on the matter."

Maeve drank some whiskey. "Did I ever tell you about Frankl when I was working on that part of my thesis?"

"Not that I recall."

"Austrian neurologist. He works with noogenic neurosis. Existential vacuum. He believes a certain type of person can experience this vacuum in every aspect of themselves. I mean, spiritually, physiologically, and psychologically. A vital low exists in all three categories, he says: loss of physical energy, generalized sense of inadequacy, and crisis in the tension between who the person is and who they believe they should be. That crisis causes the individual to lose all sense of meaning. All sense of belonging. All hope for the future."

"Sounds like you're offering our mother an awfully generous posthumous diagnosis."

"Makes some sense of her progression," Maeve said, "and why medication for sleep and nerves, for example, were ineffective. If you buy into any of his theories."

Jack felt mightily betrayed by all this. "Does anyone actually believe there's meaning to their existence? Only a fool. Not to mention, everybody thinks they should be some better way they're not, but the rest of us manage to keep carrying on, don't we? Sounds like a sorry excuse for taking the easy way out if you ask me."

Jack was scowling into his drink. He had a serious problem with the very basis of his sister's advanced degrees: that there were things in some people's brains that caused them to act in ways that were beyond their control. Unfortunately, Jack didn't feel intelligent enough to argue this point with Maeve, who would have bombarded him with supposed evidence to the contrary. But in his heart of hearts, Jack did not believe that anyone, including his mother, lacked the capacity to act right. And just to put to rest any notion of hypocrisy: Jack knew that he was one hundred percent in control of when and how much he drank. He knew when he was overdoing it; every sip was a deliberate act. He could have stopped anytime but merely made the choice not to. He would never try to say it wasn't entirely his decision, how he acted at any given moment. How pathetic would that be, to not be in control of oneself? How weak! Of course, he wouldn't get into this with Dr. Maeve and her big words and case studies.

So he pivoted to a related subject where he thought they could agree. "Still gets my goat that she didn't leave a note," he said. "Like she wanted us to wonder, to suffer *not knowing* for certain how and why she went that way, for our whole lives."

"You think you'd feel better if it was a confirmed suicide?"

"Sure. Because I *know* it was, of course, but if she'd just made it obvious, at least I wouldn't still feel lied to. And not just by her; by Wendy and Sam, too. They made up their minds to try and convince the rest of us it was a mistake. I don't really get riled up at those two about it anymore, they always just tried to protect us. She's the only one I'm really still angry at."

Maeve clarified. "You're still angry at her for leaving the door open to the chance that the overdose was a mistake."

"Aren't you? I thought we were on the same page with this."

"I guess. But I don't feel angry at her about it anymore. I don't feel much of anything toward her at all, except a sort of clinical curiosity, I can't help that, and pity."

Jack snorted. "Well yippee for you."

"Jack. I'm not being self-righteous. You know that. I'm just saying, I don't think you're doing yourself any favors still being so pissed off at her. Don't you remember the misery of her face? You think a person chooses that? Anyway, we don't need to get into this, but you might be better off allowing for the possibility that she was at the mercy of something. That's all."

No, Jack was not about to start offering allowances to his dead mother, no, thank you.

And yes, Jack remembered his mother's face. His clearest memory of it, actually, was through the passenger-side mirror in the Model T his father drove. His mother always sat in the passenger seat and the children piled into the back. Jack liked to situate himself on the passenger side so that he would have a view of his mother through the mirror because it was in these moments when Mrs. Shaw did not know she was being observed that her whole face fell differently. This mirror face always struck Jack as the truest version of his mother that he ever got to see, and so he appreciated that face, he remembered it well, for its truth, when so many other things about her felt like excuses and lies.

He drank more of his whiskey, burped, and wiped his lips on the back of his wrist. "You still seeing that painter?"

"PJ? Is that how long it's been since we've talked?"

"It hasn't been very long," Jack suggested. He didn't judge, but Maeve seemed to move through relationships very swiftly and with little emotion. Usually, from what Jack could tell, the men were considerably younger, and inferior to Maeve.

"He was a total layabout. Refused to get a real job, convinced some hotshot gallery or wealthy patron was going to take notice of his work and be his meal ticket. In the meantime though, we split entrées unless I was paying. And I had to cover his rent a couple months in a row."

Jack waved down the bartender and pointed at his and Maeve's empty whiskey tumblers.

When they both had a fresh pour, Jack said dolefully, "Why did the rest of them all end up with such losers? I don't think I could stand it if you married a loser." He didn't really think there was much danger in Maeve marrying anytime soon, period, but still.

"Not all of them. We like Anne," Maeve pointed out.

"Oh, you're right. Anne. We do. But the rest of them . . . Well, I mean, Rose is fine, too, just annoying. So I guess I'm talking about the husbands, mostly."

"We don't know Ray," Maeve said. "I've only seen him a few times since their wedding. Really don't know the guy at all."

"From everything Bette says, the guy's useless, a nincompoop."

Maeve tipped her head back and forth. "Bette's not so easy to please."

"And John Winthrop," Jack said, "that fat twat."

"Jack," she admonished. "The guy died in service. A little respect."

Jack shook his head. "Nuh-uh. I won't. I'm sorry Lane's a widow, but I hate his guts and I'm glad he's dead. I never got over the idea he did something to her. She was so young."

"She was fifteen. Plenty of girls . . . well, anyway. We've talked about this a hundred times. And back then, don't you remember? We asked her over and over, and she always maintained—"

"I know what she always maintained, but you know Lane can't stand any kind of conflict, or attention on her. She'll say anything to save anybody's hide. She never wants trouble for anybody. No matter what. Not to mention, Lane's always been such a loner. Do any of us even really know her?"

Jack finished his fish sandwich, crumpled the wax paper wrapping, and tossed it into the little red plastic basket it had been served in.

Maeve said, "I don't believe she would've left us for him if he'd actually done what you're suggesting. I really don't. And furthermore, if he had done that, and even if Lane made the decision to be with him when she was a teenager, I don't think she would've stuck by the decision for years and years after. Raised Thomas together. I don't think she could've stayed. I refuse to believe she lived with that."

Jack said, "I hope you're right." Glumly, he finished his beer. "I hope you're all right. I know everybody else is on your side on this, too."

Although there had been an initial uproar when Lane's pregnancy was revealed, and some of the others had started off firmly in Jack's corner when it came to John Winthrop, eventually, after enough time and consideration and conversation with Lane, the rest of them accepted Lane's version of events and honored her wish for a peaceful move to Chesterfield with John Winthrop. The rest of them all took Lane at her word when it came down to it. Jack would not. Could not. He knew this did not make him a hero. He didn't know what it made him.

It was quiet between Jack and Maeve for a while, though the bar was filling up and had gotten quite noisy. Some people were starting to dance. Jack didn't want things to feel wrong between him and Maeve, his favorite, his best friend. He didn't like when they were in conflict. It made his whole world feel off.

"Hoop-Dee-Doo" by Perry Como came on, and Jack started moving in his seat, beguiled by the music and able to put aside his dark thoughts about his marriage, and his mother, and John Winthrop.

Maeve began to move in her seat, too, and she sang along: *"It's got me higher than a kite, Hand me down my soup and fish, I am gonna get my wish . . ."*

Jack stood, and tugged on her elbow. "Come dance," he said.

"No way." Maeve sipped her whiskey. "You go on ahead."

"Please?"

"Nah."

Jack downed the rest of his drink in a single gulp and made his way out to the dance floor, which was not yet crowded. He shuffled back and forth and spun a few times to claim his territory, then he started to do his own comical solo rendition of the jitterbug. Elbows out and flapping, knees high. He shimmied like a woman. *"It's got me higher than a kite, Hand me down my soup and fish, I am gonna get my wish . . ."* He pantomimed the trombone solo, with flair.

He looked over toward the bar during the instrumental interlude. Maeve was still seated on her stool but she was watching him and laughing with her head tossed back, and she was clapping for him.

Jack didn't care what anyone else in the bar thought of his dancing. They could be making snide remarks, calling him a fruit, or pointing him out to the bartender, recommending that they boot him before he got wilder. Jack didn't care. They could boot him right now and he'd go willingly, happily, because he knew it didn't matter how boorish he'd gotten, how stupid, how embarrassing, how bad—Maeve would still come with him. They had arrived together, and they would leave together. Knowing this very simple fact made Jack feel so lustrous in his heart, so sure of his place in the world, that he danced even harder, kicked even higher. The music coursed through his veins and he was overtaken by ecstasy.

Camille was always accusing Jack of drinking because he didn't want to feel anything. But that wasn't right at all. Jack didn't drink because he didn't want to feel; he drank because he wanted to feel precisely this. Inalienable. Not other. He drank toward this feeling that he belonged within some ancient and eternal collective magic. An ocean, a forest, a chorus. And he belonged not because he'd been chosen, but because he simply was. How could he ever explain this to Camille? She would think it was weird, or pathetic. Who the hell cared what Camille thought? Jack would care tomorrow, or the next day, of course. He'd care, he'd lay off the booze for a while, he'd fix things, like he always did. But tonight, and hell, maybe tomorrow night, too, he would drink and he would dance.

He saluted Maeve, then leapt high and landed so low he nearly split his pants. He recovered his balance, wiggled his fingers, and sang, "*They're in clover, we're in bloom, When we're dancin', give us room . . .*"

Soldiers

1953

When Bette got pregnant, Ray decided to become certified to teach high school English, and everything in their lives improved in the months leading up to the birth. It might have been Ray's sudden ambition, his hours now spent studying for board exams instead of lounging and lamenting, it might have been that Bette's spirits were lifted by the attention and the joys and possibilities that seemed to bloom open before her, it might have been a new shared sense of purpose. In any case, laughter and goodwill returned to their home. There was an ease, tenderness, and magnanimity between them as they prepared for the arrival of the child.

Emma was a healthy baby and she took to nursing right away. It was only a few weeks before she slept soundly through the night. Bette and Ray quickly settled into a daily routine wherein she had Emma during the day while he taught, and he took an active role when he got home so that Bette could enjoy a walk or a book or a glass of wine. On the weekends, they often hosted friends or members of Ray's family for visits. A sweet and capable neighbor girl babysat when they wanted a night out.

Teaching seemed to suit Ray well. His students delighted him with their subversive ideas, and he was good at picking out novels that were to their taste. He often came home with entertaining stories from his day. Bette found that caring for a baby occupied her time and her mind in a manner that was not exactly pleasurable, but it demanded of her thoughts a certain constancy, an almost cultish adherence, and she found this grounding and gratifying.

They were startled when Bette turned up pregnant again, only six months after Emma's birth. But before they had even announced the news to family, Ray was gone.

At nine o'clock on a Saturday morning—a sunny time, a wonderful and innocent time, the last time you'd expect something to be taken from you—as he was out picking up doughnuts. Another driver ran a light at high speed and T-boned Ray in his Catalina coupe. Ray was thrown from his car, and in an instant, he was gone.

Ray's family descended on Bette with meals and childcare and logistical guidance for the funeral service. Bette traversed these days and weeks in a mangled and graceless haze, largely unaware of her words and appearance and obligations. When she passed the news along to her own family, she discouraged them from traveling for the service, which would be a large, formal, and stressful ordeal. She insisted that she'd prefer visits several months down the road, when she had her wits about her. Henry was the only one to defy her wishes by attending Ray's service. Dear Henry, the closest in age to Bette, her favorite childhood playmate and confidant. They had grown apart in adulthood. For many years Bette had been too jealous of her brother's happiness to enjoy listening to his chirpy reports of family life, and she had failed to return calls or initiate visits. Nevertheless, Bette found Henry's presence at Ray's funeral service, though brief—he didn't even spend the night—a great comfort.

Bette neglected to tell anyone of her second pregnancy until a month after Ray's funeral service, because it was believed that trauma could bring about a miscarriage and she was loath to suffer a second public tragedy in such short order. When she did finally tell Ray's parents, his mother wept powerfully. "My baby," she kept saying, "poor baby," and it wasn't clear to Bette which poor baby she was referring to; maybe all of them: Ray, Bette, Emma, and fetus.

The financial matters had already been worked out and Ray's parents wanted Bette to have everything that was already in Ray's name, which was not only the home, but stocks and bonds and savings, so that Bette was more or less set for life. Bette was deeply grateful, but she was also getting the impression that they were hopeful that all this money might incentivize her to stay in the area, and furthermore, perhaps, to not remarry.

Now, with news of the pregnancy, Ray's parents insisted that Bette accept even more of their help in some way, be it a live-in nanny on their dime, or that she actually move into their home so that Ray's mother could assist with caretaking, or perhaps that Bette move into a new home in their neighborhood so that she could at least be closer to her in-laws even if she didn't want to live under the same roof. Bette thanked them and said that she'd be all right on her own for now; she was quite settled in the house, but that she would consider their offer of a live-in nanny when the baby was born.

What Bette really longed for, oddly, were precisely the people whom she had done her best to avoid for many years: her sisters. Wendy, who always knew what to do. Maeve, who was always good for a laugh. Lane, sensitive and kind. Bette and Lane had not been particularly close at any stage of life, but Lane had offered very comforting words to Bette when she first learned of Ray's death. Lane had lost her own husband, John Winthrop, a number of years earlier, to the war, and Lane had remained a widow since, raising her son, Thomas, now a teenager, on her own. Bette longed for the presence of all, or any, of her sisters, whose attempts to remain in touch Bette had casually cast aside over the years. She longed for the familiarity, the immediate and unceremonious intimacy of sisterhood. Dared she ask for a visit from any of them, after all these years? She had said *Come in a few months instead* in relation to Ray's funeral, but would any of them take that as a serious invitation—given that it was the first invitation Bette had issued since her wedding? Dared she follow up? Suggest some dates, even? She thought she might dare to do this. And yet, weeks passed, and she did not.

Months later, the time came for Bette to empty out Ray's study so that she would have another room available, since the pregnancy seemed to be progressing healthily. She had barely set foot in the study since his death.

She decided that she would keep the shelving and his desk in there for the time being, but would empty its drawers and cabinets and declutter. Ray was not very organized, and Bette feared there could be important insurance or financial documents scattered among the tabloid magazines and old newspapers he kept in and around his desk. So she had to go through his papers slowly to guarantee that she would not discard anything essential.

Among the junk, she discovered an overstuffed manila folder filled with rejections from all sorts of literary journals, agents, and publishing houses. There were hundreds. Some related to poems or short stories or essays that Ray had submitted for publication. Some regarded proposals for full books. Some dated all the way back to before they were married, some as recent as the final month of his life. Bette sorted them by date, laid them out on the floor before her, and stared. She'd had no idea that Ray was trying so hard. He always checked the mail, and had never once left one of these out for her to open or to see. He must have always plucked these letters from the bunch and pocketed them before entering the house, then gone into his study to open them in private.

Many of the rejection letters included Ray's submission letter (or a photocopied version). In the earlier versions, Ray touted his degree, his one prior publication, and described himself as "promising," "emerging," an "important voice," "Salingeresque." In more recent letters, Ray described himself as a father, a husband, and a teacher, who had "not quite yet" given up on his lifelong dream to see his work in print one day. He thanked the reader for their time.

Bette couldn't bring herself to read any of his actual submissions, though she had already located a second manila folder in the same drawer that appeared to contain much of his work.

She didn't know Ray had written poems.

She pictured him closing the door to this room after retrieving the mail, so that he could open the letter in private. None of them were ripped haphazardly; all of the envelopes had been carefully pared open, with a blade, and now she pictured him jimmying the envelope carefully, in case it contained good news and he might want to frame it. Again and again, he had done this, hundreds of times, and never once had he shared the news, his private struggle, with Bette. As she thought about this, she felt something violent and unbearable, like her soul was being scraped out of her.

She dialed Lane, who said, "I've been thinking about you. I'm glad you called."

They chatted weather and family and recipes for a while, before Bette worked up the courage to cry. She explained to her sister that there were different categories of her daily sadness. There was missing him, an emptiness, a home that felt incomplete. There were fears for the future. There were regrets for every low and ugly opinion she'd ever held of him and every ugly word she'd spoken to, or about, him. And perhaps most painfully of all, Bette said, there were things she hadn't noticed, known, or understood about him, until he was gone.

Lane said that she related to all of this, and that all would diminish with time.

Bette said, "Even that last one?"

Lane was quiet for so long that Bette thought they might have been disconnected. Then finally Lane said in a voice that was laced with a coldness that shocked Bette: "I think sometimes you wrestle as long as you must with something. And then somehow you just find a way to end the fight, whether or not you think you've won it, because your heart just can't take any more."

Bette wanted to know more. She wanted to hear what wrestle Lane had ended with her dead husband, or perhaps with herself, without knowing if she had won.

Yet they had to end the call, because Emma had woken from her nap in the other room. Before hanging up, Bette thanked Lane for talking and once again encouraged her to come for a visit, anytime, and she reiterated that Lane's son, Thomas, was welcome, too.

Lane's voice changed back to itself when she said, "I just might."

Bette went to Emma's room and lifted her from her crib. She bounced her until she settled, and then carried her into Ray's study where all his rejections were still spread out on the floor. It occurred to her that Ray might very well still have submissions out in the world, and that more rejections would be arriving in the mail in the coming days. Or maybe an acceptance letter, his first.

What could she ever teach Emma or the unborn child about life, when she had gotten so much wrong? All she knew now was that she had to figure out a way to carry on despite her failures, the same way Ray had carried on despite his. So perhaps one day Bette would be able to teach them this: that you must somehow find a way in life to forgive your own heart for the ways it has failed you; for the ugliness of the things you'd thought and said and done and felt, in order to forge ahead. Yes, that's what she would say. See, your heart was a bleeding soldier and you simply had to give it whatever it needed, in order to keep it marching on.

Ocean

1932

Lane's love of reading took hold when her schoolteacher intro-
duced her to literature from centuries past; it seemed to Lane that
in older novels, the skin of a story was more transparent. She read
these books at home, in the grass, while ants traveled over her bare
legs, and her mind soared. A mysterious thing happened, though.
Lane realized that the more she read, the slower a reader she was
becoming. At first she thought it might be a lack of focus, so she
decided to pursue each thought she had while reading to its final
destination, to learn the source of her distraction. She discovered
that it wasn't outside intrusions that slowed her reading, but an
almost fanatical preoccupation with unnamed and inconsequen-
tial people in books. A bearded gardener with a bent back; a pale
woman who stood with a horse, mentioned only once and in passing. In her mind, Lane realized, she lingered on these people long
after they had served their purpose in the book. She knew this was
no author's intention. But why shouldn't she linger? Each of these

people was a protagonist, too, Lane thought, in their own mind and their own life; it just so happened that their novels remained unwritten. This idea gave rise to all sorts of magical thinking. For example: if Lane herself were to appear in a novel, she wondered, as a quiet girl reading old books in the grass, would any reader, a hundred years from now, linger on her? Would she disappear in the reader's mind as quick as a drop into an ocean? Or would she reach out from the spine of the book to take the reader by their hand, or by their throat?

The Decent Thing

Several months had passed since the death of her husband, John Winthrop, and Lane had since gotten a part-time job at the library in Chesterfield, accepted many casseroles and condolences, and emptied the house of his things. John's mother had insisted that none of John's belongings be discarded; not a nearly empty canister of shaving cream, not a sock without a match. So Lane had boxed these items and taken them to her in-laws' home, the same house where she and John had lived together when she was pregnant with Thomas and they first moved to the area. She hadn't a clue what Mrs. Winthrop intended to do with this junk.

Thomas was eleven years old now, a slight and agreeable boy. He had not immediately cried at the news of his father's death, nor, a year earlier, at the news that his father had been drafted for service and would be leaving. In both cases he cried eventually, but not immediately. Lane saw so much of herself in Thomas. It had always taken her a long time to arrive at reactions, too. Fortunately, these days, books seemed to occupy Thomas and bring him solace. He devoured the novels Lane brought home from the library for him.

One afternoon on her way home from her shift at the library, Lane was jolted out of a sun-warmed, thoughtless daze, by something along the side of the road. Unreasonably, her first thought was, *A baby!?* Not because of the shape or color, but there was something about the wrongness of it, the vulnerability, that inspired this panicked thought. She pulled her car onto the shoulder of the country road, both sides flanked by rolling cornfields and little else, and got out. She approached the object and it did not take long to see that it was in fact not a baby, but a small yellow dog.

"Oh no." Lane drew her breath in sharply. It was on its side, clearly dead. There was a bit of blood caked around its open mouth. It did not wear a collar. "Oh no," Lane said again. She didn't know what to do.

A rumbling alerted her to an approaching vehicle, and she moved farther onto the shoulder of the road to allow it to pass. But it was a tractor, not a car, so it moved slowly, and it did not pass but slowed when it drew near, and stopped behind Lane's car where it was parked. The tractor was a red Farmall, like the tractor Lane's father used. The driver dismounted. He was about her age, mid-twenties, with round eyes.

He waved in a friendly manner and called out, "You in some kind of car trouble, ma'am?"

"No," Lane said, and she gestured down at the dog on the ground.

"Oh," the man said, and he walked, then ran, for a closer look. "Oh no," he said, falling to his knees next to the dog.

Lane thought, *Oh no*. He knows this dog.

The man tugged at his hair with both hands, in distress, and he said, "Otis, Otis." He knelt closer to the animal and placed his fingers on the dog's little rib cage to make sure there was no pulse. He smoothed the fur on the dog's nose. He sniffed.

"He belongs to my daughter," he said without looking up. "This is going to . . . Oh God, she'll be . . . She's had Otis since he was a pup."

"I'm so sorry," Lane said.

The man fixed his gaze on Lane, and then to her surprise, scowled. He said, "You should be. Matter of fact, you might want to tell her so yourself. My daughter, I mean. That'd be the decent thing."

"What?" Lane said.

"What was your plan, pulling over after you ran him over? Kick him into the ditch so the owner'd never find him, then be on your way?"

"No, no," Lane said, using both hands to explain. "*I* didn't hit him. I saw him on the side of the road and stopped because I thought it might be a baby."

The man snorted. "A baby?"

"Sounds stupid to say now," Lane said. She didn't know why

she had mentioned this at all, about the baby. "I saw something that didn't look right, so I pulled over only a minute before you got here yourself. I swear I didn't hit your dog. I didn't kill Otis."

The man rose to his feet and made his way over to Lane's car, where he took a close look at the front bumper and both front tires, even running an index finger along these surfaces.

Eventually he seemed satisfied with what he saw, or didn't, and he gave Lane a sheepish look. "I owe you an apology," he said. "I oughtn't've assumed. It's just, the city folk tend to drive way too fast on this road. Makes me mad. Things like this happen when you drive too fast on a road."

"I completely agree," Lane said, still a little miffed but also relieved that this had not turned into more of an ordeal. "I personally don't drive fast," she added. She was ready to be on her way now.

The man looked back down at Otis. "Listen," he said, in a voice that was now spiked with a plea. "Like I said, my daughter's real attached. We got Otis not long after my wife passed." He paused. "In childbirth," he added.

"I'm sorry," Lane said.

"So it's just been me and my daughter a couple years. And Otis."

Lane didn't know what to say.

The man coughed. He had grease on one cheek. "It's not right for me to ask," he said, "but, telling her this news . . . it's gonna kill me. I can't bear the thought." He stared off into the distance then continued, turning to face Lane. "She's at home with my mom, who looks after her most days while I'm at work," he said. "Is there any chance . . . I've got a job to do, I'm not meant to return home till five." He paused again, fiddled with a button on his shirt. "My house is just over this next hill, first house you'll see. Any chance you'd go there now and tell them about the dead dog? You don't have to make like you did it, obviously, but maybe just knock on the door and tell them there's a dead dog, little yellow thing, out here on the street, and you're just knocking on nearby doors to try and alert the owner. Just so they already know by the time I get home. So I don't have to be the one to tell my daughter, or be there when she finds out. Would you do it for me?"

Lane didn't know what to say. Otis was not her fault. This man's daughter was not her daughter. She did not want anything to do with this mess.

She sighed. "Which one is your house?"

The man practically collapsed with relief. "Oh, thank you, ma'am, I can't thank you enough. It's the white one on the left, first house you'll pass up thataway. I really can't thank you enough." He put his palms together, long fingers, like a conspiring rodent. He said, "You'll do a better job of this than I would."

Lane said, "Well then." She got into her car and pulled back onto the road.

Months earlier, a representative from the Department of the Navy had come to Lane's house to inform her of the death of her husband, John Winthrop. Thomas was at school, so she had received the news alone. They had a nice thing written up already, which the representative told her she was free to edit for the official obituary. It described John as a "respected member of the U.S. Marine Corps," a "devoted husband and father" and "beloved son." Lane didn't know where they had gotten this information, but she supposed John was all of these things. Yes, he definitely was. But he was also that other thing, too.

It had taken Lane a long time to heal from Thomas's birth, and she battled several infections resulting from the episiotomy. Eventually, she was deemed fully healed, and the doctor gave her the go-ahead to resume sexual relations with her husband. But when John asked her about her appointment that evening at dinner, she didn't tell him this part of it. Instead, she reported that her doctor had said things would probably never be normal for her, down there. There would always be a high risk of infection. It would never not be dangerous.

This was the most direct thing she had ever said to John, in that department. While he knew that she was having some medical problems with her recovery from labor, and had not pushed for any sexual contact, Lane could tell he was becoming curious about a timeline.

"Never not be dangerous?" John said. "What does that mean?"

"That we can't safely have that sort of relation," Lane said.

"Ever. I'm sorry." She lifted a napkin to her eyes to disguise the fact that there were no tears.

"*Never?* Oh no, no, don't cry," John said. "It's not your fault." He covered his face. It was clear to her that he was crushed by this news and trying to conceal his tears as she was trying to manufacture some of her own.

Some time later, once Thomas was no longer nursing every few hours, John began to kiss Lane in bed in a more insistent way. Eventually, he worked his way up to pleasuring himself with her hand, which she did not enjoy, but she could tolerate it. Sometimes he made moves to try to pleasure her, too—never roughly— but she always squirmed away. There was no pleasure that he could possibly make in her. Because although at that time Lane was still not entirely clear on what had happened on the occasion of Thomas's conception, a memory was starting to take form and take hold of her.

It wasn't until years later that the curtain in Lane's mind was finally lifted and the memory fully brought forth on one sleepless but otherwise unremarkable night. The memory in all its gruesome clarity descended upon and then encased Lane, like concrete, so that she was cold and immobile and trapped inside of the memory, instead of the other way around. She had always known, of course.

And John had to know that she knew—there was no way that her behavior toward him had not undergone a fundamental change when she remembered—but he never once owned up to what he had done. Never looked it in the eye. To be fair to John, he had never repeated the behavior, not even remotely; it was almost like he'd gotten it out of his system. He was a devoted husband and father, this was true. And yet.

As the Department of the Navy representative offered Lane his sincerest condolences on the death of her devoted husband, he added, "Times like this, ma'am, I hardly know what to say. Sometimes there are no words."

Lane thought, *That's not true.* There was a word for everything. It was just that sometimes it took a very long time before you would, or could, use the right word, even with yourself, even in the privacy of your own heart.

Lane crested the hill of the country road, and spotted a dilapidated white farmhouse on the left side of the road. She thought of the tractor-driving man's implication that to comfort and reassure was not only her womanly gift but her womanly duty; that, even though she'd never before even set eyes on this man's daughter, it fell on her to deliver gentle, false words, to make everything right.

Lane slowed as she approached the driveway. The mailbox was a sad, crooked thing, the front flower beds were badly in need of some care. But then she thought, *No! No! No! No! No!*, and she hit the gas hard and sped on ahead without even giving the house another look. She felt suddenly wonderful. A burst, something fixed. It was not her job to make things right for that man and his child. Let him deal with it himself, for once.

Visitations

1929

Jim retrieved a plump Fraser fir several weeks before Christmas, at the urging of his children. They watched, and offered many opinions as he trimmed the tree for shape with the same shears he used on the hogs' hooves. It was very cold and overcast and had not snowed, though the air smelled of it. The rolling landscape was brown and bluish.

Wendy wanted to pop corn for the little ones to string onto long decorative threads for the tree, which they had done in the past, but her parents forbade it, citing the waste. It had not been a good year. The yield had been fine, but the market had crashed at the end of summer and Jim had been forced to accept a meager price. Wendy had observed with interest the way her father's body was transformed by this whole ordeal, his long neck curling and shoulders gathering in, so that now he had the shape of a weasel whereas before he stood proud. Given the recent state of things, Wendy supposed she ought to be pleasantly surprised to have a

Christmas tree in the house at all, and she was, though it didn't make any sense to her that it should remain unadorned. Instead of popcorn, then, Wendy suggested that they gather little novelties from outdoors to decorate the tree. She sent her siblings out with buckets. They returned with dried reeds and stems that they tied into loose bows around the tree's branches, and pine cones and puffed brown cattails that they balanced on its thicker boughs.

Wendy had overheard recent talk between Mr. and Mrs. Shaw of trying to sell off some land or livestock. But who had money to buy? They would only get bottom dollar, then find themselves without assets when the market returned, if the market returned. Nobody knew what to expect; they had not seen a crash like this in their lifetimes. In any event, Mrs. Shaw had announced early in the month that Christmas presents would not be exchanged this year, and the children knew better than to grumble when their mother's voice took on that pinched sound, like it was being squeezed through a too-small tube.

But Wendy couldn't stand the thought of a Christmas without presents any more than she could stand a bare tree. So she took a pocket knife into the woods and returned with branches of beech, which she had secretly been whittling into animal figurines to give to her siblings, working every evening in the bedroom she shared with her sisters after they went to sleep. She had never been taught to whittle but had seen it done years ago by an artisan in town and was having some success now, mimicking his technique. She started the first one with plans for a bear but shaved too thin around the neck, so the bear became a cat, and then when she nicked an ear off, a bird. She was careful to clean up the curled trimmings that littered the floor next to her bed every night.

When she had finished all six animals, Wendy lined them up next to one another on the windowsill to assess her work. The hound kept falling over. Individually, the animals were unimpressive. Small heads and strange, macabre faces. As a collection, though, there was a certain consistency to her work that rendered it more stylish, she thought. The fox was the best; it was the last one she had completed and the progression of her skill was apparent. She'd give that one to Lane, who was the most likely to notice fine details.

It occurred to Wendy that she might become quite good at sculpting with some more practice. It would be strange to be good at something. She was accustomed to being useful, not good, which was why she had been kept out of school. The little ones marveled at the fact that their eldest sister, who was pretty much a grown-up in their eyes, could not read. "But it's so easy!" Bette and Henry would cry in delight as they shoved their lesson books before Wendy's face and pointed to letters. "Why don't you understand? Just *look!* A . . . B . . ." Wendy ignored them when they were like this because she knew they weren't trying to be mean. Also, this behavior failed to upset Wendy because in fact, in secret, she *was* learning to read, by herself and in private, and she was already at a fourth-grade level, not that far behind others her age who had been in school all along. She just didn't want help or oversight, and she didn't want her mother finding out that she was putting time toward this. Well anyway, maybe on top of being self-educated, she would become an artisan like that man in town, a master of something beautiful and interesting. Maybe then her family would admire her rather than need her.

She would wait to disperse the gifts under the tree until the night before Christmas, as a surprise.

But the next afternoon, still several days prior to Christmas, Jack was so agitated he kicked one of the barn cats, which sent Bette into hysterics, and Wendy decided to hand out the presents early to bring everyone some cheer.

Mrs. Shaw looked on silently while the children opened the gifts. She took Henry's bird and examined it up close, picked at a rough, unfinished spot with her fingernail, then tossed it back and left the room.

The children conducted some fights and races and other competitions between their animals. Even Sam, who had outgrown imaginary activities, participated politely, and Wendy felt a swell of kinship toward her brother. She could see that Sam recognized her effort and was being overly appreciative of a mediocre gift, and this touched Wendy unexpectedly. She felt a way she'd not felt before, that she and Sam were something different from the others; they were distinct, and together. From here on out, she and Sam would be a team.

Eventually, Lane suggested they use the string from the wrappings to hang their animals from the tree, like Christmas ornaments. As Wendy helped arrange the animals on the tree, she noticed a few small speckled yellow worms on its inner boughs. Then she noticed a few more. Later when she was alone, she collected all of the worms she could find, a dozen or so, plucking their sticky bodies from the sticky branches. She took them outside and smashed them under her boot.

On Christmas Eve morning, Mrs. Shaw supervised and looked on while Wendy boiled oats in water, then peeled potatoes, then spatchcocked a turkey and rubbed dried herbs and pepper into the skin. She mixed dough for molasses cookies and shaped it into balls. The turkey and cookies were for tomorrow. Meals today would be simple, the usual: oats, starchy soup, buttered bread.

Wendy gazed through the window above the sink. She could see out to the pasture, where her father was applying ointment to one of the milking cows that had a gangrenous teat. He stroked her side. Of course Wendy could not hear him now, but she knew that sometimes he spoke gently to his animals.

Snow had fallen heavily and a few inches accumulated in the night. The fields were white and glittering. It was a beautiful day, and a good day, Wendy thought.

Henry was the first of the little ones to wake. He appeared in the kitchen in his nightclothes and with crooked hair, noticed that the kitchen was in disarray and asked if they were making waffles or some other kind of a special breakfast.

Her mother didn't turn around but said over her shoulder, "Sure thing, and for lunch, it'll be ice cream sundaes."

Wendy watched as her brother's face flickered with a short-lived thrill until he realized it was a joke. Well actually, it was a mean lie. Her mother got this way, edgy and sardonic and even downright cruel, from time to time. Her father blamed it on changes to her medication, and it was true; changes to her mother's demeanor did often coincide with a recent trip to the doctor, but in Wendy's mind this was no excuse. Wendy had seen her mother cycle through all sorts of ways over the years; as timid as a newborn kitten, volatile and combative, melodramatic, lethargic, bedridden, simpering and self-pitying, and on rare occasion, nurturing and kind and self-possessed. Her father had always maintained that this last version, the best one, was the only true version of his wife, a notion that Wendy personally found ridiculous and insulting. Wendy had never once in her life found herself unable to control her emotions, or unable to care for her younger siblings when the need arose. Sure there were times Wendy was tempted to act out or eschew responsibilities, but she always exerted power over her negative impulses. Medication or not, Wendy did not believe that multiple versions of one person could exist. She simply believed that there were strong people and weak people.

✦ ✦ ✦

Wendy said to Henry, "The special meal will be tomorrow, we're just getting a head start today," and she patted his head when she delivered his oats. She didn't want him to push the issue. On top of not having the proper ingredients for waffles—they had just used the last of the baking powder for the cookie dough—the waffle maker was a sore subject.

It had been purchased from a traveling salesman this past summer, merely a few months before the crash, on a hot afternoon when Mr. Shaw was not in the house. The salesman parked a shiny red Chrysler DeSoto out front and walked into the house with a clipboard under his arm.

Mrs. Shaw offered coffee, then sat with him at the table as the salesman talked about all the implements he had for sale, of which the waffle maker was one of the most expensive. Once Mrs. Shaw had made her decision, the salesman retrieved the waffle maker in a box from the trunk of his car. He was sweating and smiling and didn't even count the cash she handed him.

When Mrs. Shaw got out the electric waffle maker to use several days later, Mr. Shaw eyed the thing and pressed her lightly on how much she had paid for it.

Wendy watched her mother lie.

It was clear Mr. Shaw thought that even the fake price his wife quoted was far too high, but he wasn't going to fight about it. Wendy knew that her mother had been born in the city of Baltimore, was educated, and had come from money. She knew that her father had grown up in the farmhouse they currently lived in, and his own parents had struggled to make ends meet. Aside from these basics, Mrs. Shaw was tight-lipped about her upbringing, and Mr. Shaw seemed to think his own background did not merit conversation. So Wendy knew little else about her parents' early years and saw little evidence of their lives before the here and now, except that when Mrs. Shaw was in a certain mood, she could be shockingly reckless with money in a way that hinted at her privileged upbringing. It was clear that Mr. Shaw disapproved, but did not fuss about his wife's spending.

The trouble with the waffle maker had gotten even worse, though, after Mr. Shaw learned of it. The thing had sparked when Mrs. Shaw plugged it in, and it had been impossible to properly modulate the heat; no matter what she tried, the waffles came out alternately either blackened or spilling runny dough from their centers. Wendy had suggested that they use the same batter to just make pancakes in a cast iron pan instead. Mrs. Shaw ripped the cord of the waffle maker out of the wall. She wept like a child as Mr. Shaw escorted her calmly to their bedroom, and on his way, he told Wendy, yes, to please go ahead and make pancakes with the remaining batter.

Apparently Henry had somehow forgotten about the whole waffle fiasco. In fairness, it was difficult to remember every single one of Mrs. Shaw's fits and moods and dark spells and sick times; or at least to distinguish one from another in your mind.

✦ ✦ ✦

On the afternoon of Christmas Eve, Mr. Shaw walked with the children to the pond. He stomped across to test the ice, then he and Sam shoveled off the surface while the others scooted in their boots. The family only had three pairs of skates, so the children passed them around and everyone got a turn except for Wendy, whose feet were too big for even the biggest pair. Maeve was naturally balanced and athletic, a far better skater than the rest of them, who wobbled along, legs akimbo, in short, uneven, slapping strides. After skating, they built a snowman, then destroyed it, pelted one another with snowballs, ground their backs down all the way to the dirt making snow angels.

Inside, they laid their wet clothing out before the fire and ate soup for dinner, then set up a jigsaw puzzle and worked on it around the table. Wendy went to the tree and discreetly checked for yellow worms. She had been doing this several times a day since she first discovered them. She didn't look too hard or spend too long at it, but found and removed a small handful of them each time. Afterward, her palm always smelled sick, a little like pear.

By dusk, it was snowing heavily once again.

Around seven o'clock, there was a knock at the door. It seemed friendly enough, or not forceful, anyway. But it was startling and sent some sort of fear crackling through the house simply because they were so unaccustomed to visitors, especially after dark.

Traveling salesmen did not come since the crash, and others always planned visits in advance.

Henry whispered, "Santa?"

Mr. Shaw answered the door. It was not Santa, but a lean young man with bright cheeks and snow in his hair. He stood far back from the entryway when Mr. Shaw opened the door to make it clear that he would not enter without an invitation. Mr. Shaw looked him up and down and gazed out over the boy's shoulder where a black Ford Model T was parked. It was in bad condition.

"Beg your pardon," the young man said. "Especially on the holiday and all. Terribly sorry to intrude. I'm in a bit of a bind, and saw your light from the road."

Mr. Shaw moved to the side to permit the young man entry. He closed the door behind him.

The young man brushed snow from his hair and gazed in at the rest of the family, who were gathered around the table working on the puzzle except for Sam and Jack, who were playing checkers.

Mr. Shaw said, "Nasty weather to be on the road."

"When I left this morning, I was expecting to beat the snow."

"Where you headed?"

"Northbound, to Clayborne. It's where my granny lives. I was headed there for the holiday, planned on getting in before sundown, but got waylaid by the squalls." He offered his gloved hand. "Liam."

"Jim Shaw. You're a long way from Clayborne, son."

"I was afraid of that. I can hardly make heads or tails, east from west, with the snow. I'm meant to stay on 613 most of the way, but I got nervous all the sudden I'd taken a wrong turn. I've made the trip enough times, I didn't even bring a map. So when I saw a light, I thought I'd come and make sure I'm still on the right route, and see how far I've got ahead of me so's I'm prepared."

"That's 613 right out there. But a long way is what you've got ahead of you," Mr. Shaw said. "At least three hours to Clayborne and that's traveling at normal speed. And in this?"

The pink was fading from the young man's cheeks. His features were very cute, Wendy thought, like a baby animal.

"Well, I won't be imposing anymore, then," he said. "I'm relieved to know I didn't somehow get myself off the right track. Thank you, sir, and merry Christmas."

Wendy watched her father closely as he gazed with concern back out the window. He said, "It's really coming down out there, son. Would you like to knock off here for the night, finish the drive in the morning when you've got daylight on your side?"

"Oh . . ."

Liam's eyes darted over to the children, who were all staring, transfixed by the interaction. When his gaze passed over Wendy, her face burned with something like shame, though she didn't know why she should feel that of all things. *He* was the one imposing. She should have felt calm, but she didn't—all her insides felt like a storm.

Liam said to Mr. Shaw, "I really couldn't, with the holiday and all."

It was obvious he wanted to accept the invitation, the only question was how long he would continue to pretend he didn't.

Mrs. Shaw said, "Let me fix you some soup, it'll still be warm. We don't have a guest room, but can set you up with blankets on the couch."

Further evidence in Wendy's mind that her mother's condition was within her control: it was clear that her mother was categorically a better woman to everyone outside of the family. Mrs. Shaw demonstrated far more energy to impress, more warmth and more generosity for a stranger, than for her own children.

Liam eventually relented, and he removed his coat and gloves.

As he ate his soup, Liam answered Mr. and Mrs. Shaw's polite questions about his family and his home and life. The children didn't even bother pretending the puzzle, or checkers, held half the intrigue of this strange visitation. They suspended all their activities and instead listened, spellbound, to the stranger's small talk.

In truth, Wendy thought, Liam's conversation was not very interesting at all. He worked long hours at an automobile plant in Winston-Salem, his parents had both passed so his granny was his only family, and he got up to see her every year around the holidays.

Eventually, Henry said, "Have you got a dog?"

Mrs. Shaw said, "What's that got to do with anything?"

"Yes, I do," Liam said, turning to face Henry. "A little Scottie. His name's Alexander."

Henry said, "Alexander."

Encouraged by Henry's success, Bette asked, "What about a cat?"

"No cat," Liam said.

They chatted around the table a bit longer and then it was time for bed. Mr. Shaw added wood to the fire, and the children gathered their clothing from the floor where it was drying. Liam thanked Mrs. Shaw for the delicious soup, which Wendy had made.

Wendy lay awake in her bed for a while, thinking about the young man on their couch. Was he asleep already? Had he removed his pants? His socks? Would he stay for breakfast? The house seemed like a completely different place with a stranger in its midst; its dimensions had changed, every sound and smell was magnified, and a little off. Would he add wood to the fire when it got low? What would he tell his granny tomorrow, about the family he had stayed with? Would he remember all their names?

What about now, was he asleep now?

Wendy was woken by shrieking just before dawn. She bounded downstairs in her nightgown. Her parents were in the kitchen, where all the cabinets were ajar, and many were empty. She glanced into the living room where the couch was also empty, the blankets folded neatly at the foot. She looked outside; the car was gone. It was no longer snowing.

Mrs. Shaw beat weakly at her husband's chest and he tried to console her. Wendy sucked in her breath. "Did he . . ."

"The nice china," her mother wheezed. "The pop-up toaster."

Mr. Shaw's face was red and gnarled, like it had been boiled. He held his wife tight as a straitjacket while she hiccuped in his arms.

Wendy felt panic sputter through her.

Lane appeared in the doorway of the kitchen. "What's happening?" she said. "Where's Liam?"

Wendy spoke bluntly, "He's gone. He stole everything and he's gone."

Lane's eyes grew wide and watery. She moved stiffly through the kitchen, careful to stay well out of her mother's way, then into the living room. She stood over the couch where Liam had lain to rest.

Wendy remained in the kitchen for a few minutes, quietly assessing everything that was gone, and everything that remained. The everyday tableware was still there, as were all the mixing bowls, the spatulas, the whisks. She opened the refrigerator, where their Christmas turkey and the cookie dough were untouched. The spices and pantry items, he had left behind. He hadn't taken cutlery, nor the knife block. Everything they actually needed, Wendy thought, was still here. He'd taken only the expensive, extraneous things; the newfangled things that her mother had probably spent way too much money on. Christmas dinner would not be ruined.

As Wendy made her way around the kitchen a second time, she suddenly realized that in fact he had taken all the nice electric appliances except one: in the cabinet next to the sink, where months earlier Wendy had packed it back into its box after the terrible incident, was the waffle maker. A peal of laughter bubbled up within Wendy. Of course he had left the waffle maker behind! A stupid item, a pointless object, it did not even appeal to a thief.

Lane's voice carried out from the living room even though she didn't particularly seem to be addressing anyone, merely speaking aloud: "He took my fox."

Wendy went to Lane and stood by her side, next to the tree.

Lane pointed. "It was hanging right there. I can't believe he took my fox."

A yellow speckled worm was suspended from one of the pine cones on the tree, near where Lane was pointing, and when Wendy looked closer, she could see a second worm emerging from the pine cone's woody petals. Lane noticed the worms at the same time Wendy did.

"Gross," Lane said. "Are those—"

Wendy said, "Shh."

So the worms were coming from the pine cones, not the tree. Wendy felt some relief at identifying the source, because now she understood that she could simply get rid of the pine cones and the problem would be solved. She turned to Lane and said, "I'll make you a new fox. Why don't you go back to bed for a few minutes?"

She gestured over her shoulder, in the direction of the kitchen. "It's going to take him a while to calm her down."

After Lane left, Wendy began to collect the pine cones from the tree but to her dismay, more and more yellow worms materialized. Not just on the pine cones. They were everywhere. Dozens. No, hundreds. In some places they were bunched together into a singular squirming mass. Larvae. *Sawflies.* They were everywhere. This was not going to be some easy fix. The whole tree had to go before they hatched and filled the house.

Wendy removed the rest of the animal figurines from the tree and tossed them onto the couch. She would wait for her father to carry her mother to their bedroom, which was inevitable, then she would drag this wretched tree outside herself. She wished Sam was there to help her, but she wouldn't wake him. Her brothers and sisters would be sad to find the tree gone on Christmas morning, along with everything else that had been taken in the night, but it simply had to go.

Wendy stood before the tree with her back to the kitchen, listening to her father as he spoke tenderly to her mother, who wailed like an animal. Sometimes Wendy wished that instead of speaking tenderly, her father would just give her mother a smack.

As she gazed at the tree, Wendy's thoughts turned to Liam (or whatever his name was). She pictured him looking over all the figurines last night in the low golden light of the fire, his baby-animal face deep in concentration, examining all of them and deciding the fox was the best of the bunch. She wondered if he would sell the fox, along with the china and all the appliances, and if so, if the fox would fetch a good price. She wondered if he would claim to potential buyers that he had whittled it himself; if he'd enjoy taking credit for her work. Or perhaps, she thought, suddenly rapturous at this possibility, perhaps he didn't plan to sell the fox at all, but liked it so much that he would instead keep it for himself.

Several minutes later, when she removed the tree, Wendy would find that the fox had simply dropped to the ground, and she would return it to a very happy Lane. But for now she enjoyed the thought that the young man had admired her work so much, he thought it so fine, that he simply had to have it. She reveled in this idea as she watched the writhing of the yellow worms within the tree and waited for her parents to leave the kitchen, to go upstairs, to go away, so that she could take care of this mess.

Just a Guess

1946

Bette would not be coming home. A weekend in Richmond had led to a trip up to New York City with the hope of a modeling contract, or even some acting opportunities. The trip to New York City had led to a date with a young man she met there, which led to more dates and a trip to Philadelphia to meet his family. And this had led to a quick engagement.

Wendy was not shocked by this development. Ever since she was a young girl, Bette had been a person whose charm seemed to be reserved and cultivated primarily for romantic pursuits. And Bette had clearly been anxious to leave home as soon as Henry left for college. Still, even though it did not come as a surprise, it saddened Wendy that her final sibling's departure happened so quickly and that Bette had so little emotion about leaving home, and so little desire to return once her decision had been made. In fact, Bette had asked Wendy to send many of her belongings by post to eliminate the need for a final trip home.

And then there was Bette's wedding. The invitations were beautifully embossed and made clear that formal attire was expected. Wendy called Bette for advice on clothing and when Bette did not return the call, Wendy consulted both Maeve and Lane. The three sisters were the only Shaw family members to attend Bette's wedding; Sam and Jack were in service, Henry intended to be there but ran into car trouble that he wasn't able to sort out in time, and Mr. Shaw had sliced his leg on a barbed-wire fence: a serious infection was brewing, and his doctor forbade travel. Wendy was thrilled to see her sisters, but daunted by the festivities and formality of the occasion. She and Lane and Maeve stuck together, avoiding Ray's family and friends as much as they could. Maeve drank too much and became loud. There was an awkward moment when Bette's desire for a family picture that did not include Wendy was made clear, but Wendy did not dwell on this. Bette was young, still a child in Wendy's eyes. In fact, Wendy was so unfazed by the photograph moment that when Maeve drunkenly brought it up later that evening, saying, "Don't worry about the photo thing, Wendy, she's been such a pill all day," Wendy had already forgotten all about it.

It was November now, six months past Bette's wedding. Her father had sold off a lot of land over the years, and the fields that remained were frosted over, so tending to the animals was his only duty at present and the seasonal farmhands had all been dismissed.

He and Wendy had settled into a comfortable routine since the upheaval of Bette's departure and his leg injury (which was fully healed by now). The two of them ate breakfast together, then often did not overlap again until suppertime, as he was occupied outdoors and she kept up the house. After supper, they sat in the living room, sometimes over a puzzle, sometimes listening to records, sometimes both mending something, a curtain or a shoe, or sharpening a knife, and tending the fire to keep it bright and warm until bedtime.

Now and then, her father said things like, "I can fend for myself if you'd ever like to have a supper out sometime, with someone, now that the others are all gone. I know I'm not the greatest company. Maybe you'd like to go to the square dance. I don't know. Maybe a play."

Her father never looked at her face when he said things like this, and Wendy could always tell when one of these statements was coming because it took him several anxious hours to work up to it. She appreciated the sentiment, but Wendy had never imagined herself being courted or married. That life was like something that existed on the far side of a chasm. It ran parallel to her current life, and she could sometimes catch glimpses, and in certain ways it resembled the path she walked, yet it had never been within reach, she could never actually set foot on it.

But now that it had been six months since Bette's departure, Wendy was slipping in new ways she had not anticipated. With only herself and her father in the house, she felt an itching, aching aimlessness; a desire to wash sheets that were already clean, to cook for three, or for eight, instead of for two. At night she experienced silence and darkness more profoundly than ever before. She was acutely aware of hollow spaces in her body, such as her lungs. Her sleep was disturbed. Memories flickered through her mind too fast and too thin for her to grab hold. Holidays and beestings and horse rides and vicious fights over the first and last bite of things. The Winthrop boy, whom Wendy had never forgiven for taking Lane, and Lane's baby, so far away from the Shaw home. The secret she and Sam shared, but had never once discussed. She thought of haircuts and sprained wrists. The arrival of a new sibling, that big fiery love that felt like the whole sun was shining out of her chest, a love that was born inside Wendy right along with the baby. She wished every baby in the world were hers. Oh, what was wrong with her? Thinking about babies? She'd had her whole life to prepare for this. She'd been the first child to arrive in this house, after all, and for many, many years it had been clear that she would be the last to remain. She had always known what was coming. And yet, now that they were all gone, she started each day dizzy with emptiness.

One afternoon, Wendy's work in the kitchen was interrupted by a phone call. She dropped the dough and rinsed her hands. It was Maeve. Wendy was so ecstatic at the sound of her sister's voice that she could have jumped into the air. They small-talked for a few minutes, and Maeve remarked on the fact that Wendy and her father must be enjoying the peace and quiet of an empty house. Wendy didn't want to be pitied, so she said, "Yes."

Maeve was calling to report that she had been admitted to the PhD program where she was currently finishing her master's degree, so she would be staying in Cincinnati for the foreseeable future.

Wendy congratulated Maeve and asked about her plans for the summer.

"I'd like to get a head start on some coursework, so will probably spend most of the summer in the library. If I feel like I can get away for a couple days, or weeks, I'd like to go for a trip north, maybe check out Niagara Falls. I've always wanted to do that."

Wendy asked more about the program and Maeve's life in Cincinnati but was unable to focus as Maeve chattered about her research and her apartment, and joked indifferently about failed dating relationships. Maeve's words hovered just out of Wendy's reach; she could hear her sister's voice but the despair she felt was so thick that the language passing between them was obscured.

Recently when Wendy had been reminded that Maeve was set to graduate with her master's degree in the spring, she'd found herself nurturing a little golden ball of hope that graduation might mean Maeve would come back home. Even if it was temporary. Wendy had no real reason to think this, but she knew that Maeve was publishing papers in journals these days, and thought that perhaps Maeve would want to return to the quiet farmhouse life to do some more independent work in research and publishing for a while, before she was on to the next thing. Again, Wendy had no reason to believe this was even a consideration. But the others were all so out of reach now—Bette, Henry, and Lane all married, and Jack and Sam in service—that somehow Wendy had allowed herself to center her hopes on Maeve, and her impending graduation. And her perpetually single status. But now it was obvious that Maeve would never return. It was not on her radar, not even for a summer, not even for a day. If she was able to get away, it would be to Niagara Falls; was that what she had said?

Wendy desperately tried to react with enthusiasm that would not betray her true feelings. Maeve had done nothing wrong. Wendy was the wrong one, to hope. She asked if Maeve wanted her to retrieve their father, out in the barn, to chat, and Maeve said, "No, I need to go, you can pass along the news."

They said their goodbyes, and Wendy gazed out the window. It was raining and the sky was very dark for midday. A flock of Canada geese flashed silvery across the sky just above the tree line. One spring when they were young, the children had attempted to coax a dozen Canada geese to spend their entire season on the Shaw pond by feeding them bread every day. Unfortunately, it didn't take long for the geese to grow spoiled and gluttonous, charging at the children when they approached the pond, hissing until the bread had been distributed. On one occasion, a goose went so far as to peck Henry in the leg when he had run out of bread, and Henry was little, so this made him cry. The rest of the children acted collectively and on instinct; they all grabbed for rocks to throw or sticks to wield as weapons, and attacked not only the offending goose but all the others, too. They hadn't landed any blows, Wendy didn't think, but the geese had left the pond that day, and not returned. There was another memory in close proximity to that one and she reached for it, too, but as hard as she tried, she couldn't seem to access it fully, there were only miscellaneous shapes and shreds.

At supper that evening, Wendy told her father about Maeve's acceptance into the PhD program.

He was impressed. He seemed genuinely happy for Maeve; he did not share Wendy's reaction at all. She suspected he had been wise enough to steel himself against hopes, long ago.

Wendy didn't want to expose herself to her father—her suffering felt so unreasonable. She said neutrally, "I thought Maeve might want to come home for the summer, but apparently she has other plans."

Her father said, "Maeve's always got plans, hasn't she?" and as far as Wendy could tell, there wasn't a trace of disappointment in his voice. A moment later, he was whistling as he spread apple butter on his bread. Rain was splattering against the windows in bursts, and there was a grumble of distant thunder.

How had they all gotten off so easy, Wendy wondered of her father and her siblings, with their whistling and their plans for

Niagara Falls. How had they all escaped one another, so fully intact? Wendy knew life was not fair. Life just came at you, and kept coming. That was all there was to it. Anything beyond that, anything like hope, was just a guess.

Wendy cleared the dishes and retrieved little cups of vanilla custard from the refrigerator, for dessert.

Jim remarked, "This was your mother's very favorite thing to eat when she was pregnant. She couldn't get enough of it."

"I remember," Wendy said.

Wendy was too little when her mother was pregnant with Sam to remember that pregnancy, but she could recall all of the others, though there were many, and so some of them commingled in her thoughts. Still, she remembered the custard. And she remembered how, as a young girl, she was convinced that she, too, felt kicks in her own body. Little jolts and vibrations that meant, *I'm alive! I need you!* And since those kicks were never even hers to begin with, Wendy knew that this was even crazier yet, but she could swear that she still felt those kicks inside her sometimes, to this very day.

The Cannery

1949

Most of the men Sam had served with were taking advantage of the G.I. Bill to get their education, but Sam had received what seemed like a better offer: full-time employment at the sardine cannery his father-in-law owned and ran up in Maine, and the promise that the business would one day become his. (Sam was viewed as the natural successor since his wife did not have siblings.) Sam was initially dubious about moving to Maine because of how far it would take him from the only place he'd ever known as home, the Shaw family farmhouse in Virginia. But by now his brothers and sisters had scattered as well, all except for his older sister, Wendy, who still lived at the family home with their father. Mr. Shaw's health was starting to decline. This weighed on Sam, as did his brother Jack's drinking, and his sister Lane, who was widowed and raising her son, Thomas, on her own, down in Chesterfield. And Wendy, of course, whom Sam had always been the closest to, whose own life had been eclipsed by caretaking duties.

In any case, Sam's family gave him plenty to worry about and he disliked the idea of being so far from the family home, even as it was being sold off acre by acre; soon, Shaw land would be whittled down to little more than the driveway and the porch. But the cannery was lucrative and offered a good life. And Rose was hard to say no to. And Sam liked having things decided for him; he and Rose were a good match that way.

Rose's parents provided the down payment for a beautiful two-story home right on the water, just a few blocks from the cannery. It had a magnificent ocean view. As with the cannery job itself, Sam was reluctant to accept something he hadn't earned, but Rose convinced him these gestures were made with love, and without strings attached. Mr. and Mrs. Aird helped Sam and Rose get settled, then Sam started up work with his father-in-law.

The cannery employed packers, fishermen, and a dozen other employees who operated machinery or did maintenance. Sam spent his first week in Mr. Aird's office, looking over financials with Mr. Aird and the accounting officer, who explained the ins and outs. They also discussed branding and marketing in a manner that suggested to Sam that Mr. Aird knew little about either aspect; nevertheless, the business was enjoying steady growth. Sam did not have a background in business except for running some numbers for his father's farm long ago. He felt vastly out of his league in conversation with the accounting officer, and struggled to focus and keep up. He took many notes and studied them at home in the evenings to try to gain understanding.

Mr. Aird was an aggressively cheerful man who did not seem to be held in particularly high esteem by his employees. They were never outright disrespectful, but Sam saw the looks they exchanged when the head honcho's back was turned.

After a week of conversation in his office, Mr. Aird decided to put Sam through a crash-course training program, whereby he would work every station in order to gain fluency with overall operations. He decided that Sam should start with a week on the packing line.

Nearly all the packers were females, and most had been with the company for a long time. Sam was assigned to train with Norma, an imposing woman who routinely put up the best numbers, Mr. Aird said. Sam had noticed that Norma ate her lunch alone.

The first morning of training, Norma tossed Sam a hairnet, then grasped his bare hands with her gloved, greasy ones, looked them over, and selected a pair of women's medium-sized rubber gloves for him. She said, "I hear you're my new boss."

"No, not for some time," Sam said. "I'm learning the ropes."

"You with me all week?"

Sam nodded.

"Main thing is you don't get in my way," Norma said.

The conveyors kicked into action at eight o'clock sharp, and Sam watched with awe as Norma sorted and scooped, gripping perfectly sized and curated handfuls of fish and placing them in the small metallic cans before her, which moved along a thin belt traveling in the opposite direction as the fish. She plucked and packed with both her hands, simultaneously; she was the only one on the line who did this, and naturally, she worked at nearly twice the speed of everyone else.

She spoke coarsely over her shoulder, "You get a feel for how much to grab, so's you're not fussing around, adding or taking out, that's what'll get you speed."

Norma's large hands moved like machines perfectly calibrated to this task. She did not make mistakes, and her pace never faltered. Sam was terrified to join her on the line.

After a while a few of the packers started chatting. They had to speak loudly to be heard above the volume of the machinery. One of them was having problems with a sister-in-law. Another one's toddler kept biting other children at the nursery. They did not engage Norma in their conversation nor did she attempt to insert herself. Sam watched and listened and looked at the clock and tried to mime the action with his hands in preparation to join.

Eventually, Norma called back to him, "Time to jump in, junior."

The woman next to Norma made room, and Sam stepped forward to join the line. As he'd expected, he was terrible. Fish slipped out of his hands. He grabbed way too much on his first fistful. Overcorrected. Fumbled the can and knocked the filled one next to it askew on the belt.

Norma grunted as she reached across him to correct the mistake.

By noon, Sam had gotten only slightly better.

A bell rang, the conveyors slowed, and the packers stepped away from the line. They discarded their gloves in a bin, but did not remove their hairnets. Sam had—stupidly, he realized—put his lunch in Mr. Aird's personal refrigerator in his office, versus the fridge in the cafeteria that the rest of the staff shared, so he needed to part ways with Norma to retrieve it. He didn't want her to think he was going to eat in Mr. Aird's office like one of the higher-ups, so he said, "Gonna use the john."

Once he had his lunch, he located Norma in the cafeteria, seated alone. She ate a sandwich and stared at the wall.

Sam said, "Mind if I join?"

He sat across from her, and pulled items from his lunch box, which Rose had packed.

Norma laughed at the fact that he had both cookies and a chocolate bar. "Wife trying to fatten you up?"

"I reckon," Sam said.

"You got kids?"

"Not yet, but we hope. You?"

Norma shook her head. "We hoped, too, but."

"Sorry," Sam said. He bit into his apple and glanced at the clock. "What does your husband do for work?"

"He was in construction."

"Retired?"

"Dead as a doorknob."

Sam flushed.

Norma clarified before he had the chance to apologize for bringing up a second sore subject in such short order: "Cancer took him last year. They caught it late so he didn't suffer long." She picked her nose, and Sam looked away. "So how'd you meet Aird's daughter?" she asked.

"Flight back home to the States. I served, and she worked at a medical unit. Not the one where I was stationed, so we hadn't crossed paths, but we were seated next to each other on the plane."

Sam had returned from the war a modest hero, having taken a front line and saved lives. Carried bodies on his back even after he'd been shot in the leg. He never would have brought this up of course, but one of his fellow infantrymen was seated on the other side of him on the flight, and when he picked up on Rose's interest in Sam, he spun a great rendition for her. It humiliated Sam, who would have lacked the courage to initiate a conversation with such a pretty girl.

In the end, Rose was very taken with the tall, quiet veteran, and the bullet in his thigh.

After a few months of exchanging letters and phone calls, Rose announced that she wanted to marry. Her intentions were clear, all her feelings and desires made known. Sam could not say no to a woman like this. He never would have said so to his wife, but one of his favorite things about her was her plain speech, the straight-forwardness of her emotions. Almost like a child. How could he explain this? He'd never seen a grown woman get so excited about an ice cream, or so upset about a dead cat by the side of the road. It was a great comfort to be with a woman who said things like: *These clouds are making me feel sad today.* See, Sam did not want to marry a mystery. This was not to say Rose was some simpleton—she was very clever—but she had no darkness that could not easily be understood, and quite often set right with a simple course of action.

Norma said, "She take after her father?"

"Mr. Aird? No, no, not at all," Sam said quickly.

The afternoon passed slowly and uneventfully, and the bell rang at four o'clock. Norma walked Sam through cleanup duties and said, "Not bad for your first day," as she removed her gloves.

At supper that evening, Rose asked how his first day on the line had gone.

"I'm slow as can be," Sam said, "but they were nice. Not that they have much of a choice."

"I'm sure you were great," Rose said, "and I'm sure they all loved you." She had spent the past month trying to convince Sam that no one at the company would resent him for arriving with an elevated role.

Sam told her about Norma, who packed with both hands.

Rose said, "Oh, hon, I meant to tell you, your brother called today."

"Which one?"

"Jack."

Sam didn't hear a lot from his siblings these days. "What's he up to?" he said.

Rose looked down and swirled some applesauce around her plate. "I'm sorry to say this, but I think he was drunk."

"Ah." Sam chewed his meat slowly.

While in service, Jack had developed a reputation among his fellow infantrymen for drinking too much and starting fights. He'd been reprimanded on multiple occasions, and this news had reached Sam even though they were not stationed together. Then, after returning from the war, Jack had gone through a thing where he drunkenly called Sam often. Jack usually brought up John Winthrop, Lane's husband, who had been killed in the war, during these calls. Jack seemed to bring him up for the express purpose of saying ugly things, using John Winthrop as an excuse for coarse language and violent projections. It was very uncomfortable for Sam.

Back when Lane announced that she was pregnant, at fifteen, Sam shared Jack's initial reaction; consenting or not, Sam thought at the time, Lane was way too young. Way too small. Sam couldn't bear it, he couldn't accept it. But time passed and under intense scrutiny and interrogation from the others, Jack in particular, Lane always maintained that the act was no violation. Sam had also pushed Lane to accuse John Winthrop of a violent deed that would justify retribution, but was not nearly as demonstrative as Jack, because he was less sure. And when Lane reinforced her position again and again, Sam had increasing doubts about his own instincts. Then when Mr. Shaw told Lane that the decision was ultimately hers—where she wanted to raise the child and with whom—and she chose the Winthrops in Chesterfield, Sam accepted this as proof that her version of the events was the one they must trust. The others accepted this, too. All of them except for Jack, who never backed down with his accusations and threats toward John Winthrop; even John Winthrop's death in the line of duty had done nothing to mollify Jack. During those early postwar drunken phone calls to Sam, Jack would say all sorts of outrageous things, talk of defacing the grave, et cetera.

By now, though, it had been quite some time since Sam had fielded a drunken call from Jack. He'd been hoping those phone calls were over with and Jack had gotten himself straightened out.

"When did he call? What did he say?" Sam asked Rose nervously. Sam had always tried to protect Rose from any disturbances relating to his family. He had never described the scenario with John Winthrop and Lane to Rose with any specificity; merely that Lane had married young. So now, the idea of Jack drunkenly phoning his wife midday and possibly getting into all of that with her, was troubling.

Rose said, "It was around noon. I think he said he was calling from your sister's phone?"

"Probably," Sam said. "Far as I know, he's still staying on Maeve's couch."

"It was hard to make out much of what he was saying. Slurring his words and all. I didn't want to be rude but kept trying to ask nicely, *So . . . why are you trying to reach Sam, again?* I was just trying to figure out, did you need to call him back? Was there a message for me to pass along? Or was he just calling for a laugh, and if you called back, he wouldn't even remember calling in the first place? Anyway, eventually I just cut in and said, *Bye now, take care now,* and that was it."

Sam said, "Sorry," feeling relieved that Jack had not launched into his usual John Winthrop tirade.

"Don't be sorry for me," Rose said, reaching for his hand. "I'm just sorry he gives you cause to worry. Do you think your sister is aware?"

"Maeve's no dummy, I'm sure she knows when he's drinking too much, even if he tries to do it while she's out of the house. But she and Jack have always been so close. I imagine she sort of likes having him under her thumb so she can keep an eye on him. She's a straight shooter, and I'm sure they talk about it, but also . . . she'd never get too tough with him. Kick him out, like.

Cut him off." He lifted one shoulder. "I'm sure they'll sort it out. Reckon I'll give him a call, tomorrow, maybe."

But Sam forgot to call Jack the following evening, because the workday had ended on a bad note and he was distracted. Things with Norma had gone fine, they had eaten lunch together once again and he had done all right with his packing, but at the end of the day, Mr. Aird marched down to the line and said loudly to Norma, in front of everyone, "How's the new kid doing?"

Norma said, "Fine, sir. He's keeping up."

"Attaboy." Mr. Aird slapped Sam on the back, and then said to Norma, "Well, don't get too attached, he'll be back in the office with me next week, won't you, old boy? Might have to spend the weekend in the bathtub, get the stink off you before we have you sitting in on meetings with the bigwigs."

Mr. Aird laughed and walked away, and Sam's face burned.

Rose could tell something was bothering Sam that evening and she had to push for a while before he came out with it. He described the interaction with her father and Norma, but of course didn't point out that he had the distinct impression that Mr. Aird's employees actively despised him and Sam couldn't bear the thought of the staff resenting him, too, by association.

Rose said, "That doesn't sound like anything unpleasant to me. What's the problem?"

"He made it like I'm above the rest of them, pointing out that they do a smelly job and I'm headed to bigger, better things next week."

"Who cares?" Rose said, tossing her hands into the air. "You're so sensitive about this and I don't know why. Everybody's got things working for them or against them in life. Nobody's blaming you for marrying into the boss's family."

"I know."

"And if my dad is talking in a way that makes you uncomfortable, you should just say so, to him. He'd want you to assert yourself."

"I know." Of course Sam never would, this was not his way.

When he was a boy, sometimes Sam fought the urge to introduce himself in rooms where everyone already knew him, to say his own name out loud again and again.

Sam's third and fourth days passed without incident, and Mr. Aird did not make any more appearances on the packing line during the shift.

Sam called Maeve's house on Thursday evening, and small-talked with her for a few minutes. He learned that she had a lighter teaching load this semester and one of her papers was going to be published in a prestigious academic journal. Jack was still staying with her, though at the moment he was out to drinks with a girl he was seeing, a classmate named Camille. Sam asked how they were getting along as roommates and Maeve said that it was going well, though Jack was getting up to his normal mischief.

Sam said, "Mischief?"

"He just hits the bottle a little too hard a little too often. It's not like he's out getting himself arrested, he just gets sloppy."

"How sloppy?"

"*Silly*-sloppy, not angry-sloppy. He hasn't gotten in any fights here, if that's what you're asking."

"Rose said he called here a few days ago."

"Oh?"

"Midday. You were teaching, I assume. And I was at work. Rose said he was half in the bag when he called, and she couldn't really tell if he wanted anything. He was slurring so bad she couldn't understand anything he said."

"Uh-huh. I see," Maeve said with a tempestuous air. Sam didn't know if this was over the fact that Jack was drunk in the middle of the day and making long-distance calls from Maeve's phone, or the fact that Rose had obviously been a tattletale, a meddler, and now Sam was being one, too.

Sam said, "I just wanted to make sure everything's okay with him."

"He's fine," Maeve said. "Jack just needs extra grace, is all. You know how he is, his emotions get the best of him so easily, he needs to blow off steam a little more than the rest of us. Not to mention, *all* of you who served, it's not like that has no impact on the psyche. Gross stress reaction is what they call it. I don't know if you've talked to anybody about it, or how you're handling things, but if there are flashbacks, nightmares, hallucinations . . . All that's normal. I know loads about it."

Sam bristled at how this conversation had shifted. He said, "Nah, it's been all right for me."

"All I'm saying is that you shouldn't feel ashamed if you're having a hard time dealing with things. Serving in a war, being around death like that, has a major impact psychologically. Not telling you what to do. It's just that I study this stuff, and I hope you know it wouldn't be any sign of weakness if you felt like you wanted help."

"Jesus, Maeve," Sam said. "I'm fine. You're so worried about me all of a sudden when you should really be keeping closer tabs on the one who lives with you. I barely touch alcohol, you know. Ask Rose, ask anyone."

"Didn't mean to insult you," Maeve said.

"I know." Sam sighed, cooled down already. "You're just trying to help. Anyway, if Jack is having a hard time, you're obviously the best one for him to be staying with."

"I don't know about that," Maeve said. "I have a hard time coming down on him about anything. Even the drinking, even when it's obvious it's a problem, I just have such a soft spot for him. Can't seem to say no, can't seem to say, *You've been bad* or *You need to cool it.* I just want to see him happy and laughing all the time. It crowds out everything I know in my head to be true. Well anyhow, that's enough on that I suppose . . . How are things with you? Work? Have you started up at the cannery?"

"Yep."

"How's that going?"

Sam glanced into the other room to see if Rose was within earshot, and she was. "It's wonderful," Sam said. "Loving every minute. I really lucked out."

"That right?"

Maeve had to go soon, and they hung up.

Rose came to the kitchen and said, "Everything okay with your family?"

"Sure thing," Sam said. "All good."

At lunch on Friday, Norma said, "You must be sad it's your last day on the line."

Sam smiled. He offered her one of his cookies when he saw she didn't have a dessert today. She ate it in a single bite, then wiped crumbs from her lips. Their lunchtime conversations had gotten more personal over the course of the week, delving into politics and music and their childhoods, and Sam realized he was going to miss their lunches together.

Norma said, "This morning I woke up and made coffee for two. Doesn't happen much anymore, but sometimes I still do things like that. Make two sandwiches. Buy double the milk I need." She sniffed. "Weirdest part I guess is that I'm still doing *favors* for him, all things considered."

"How do you mean?" Sam said.

"On his deathbed, my husband told me he'd been having an affair for the past ten years. Apparently he thought he just *had* to get that out before he croaked."

Sam was gobsmacked. "Was it an apology?"

Norma nodded. "But still, why he felt the need . . . why he just had to ruin my day like that, ruin what I thought of our marriage . . . What he said was that he knew he was near death and he just had to get the truth out. It had been eating him up inside and he couldn't bear to take it to the grave." She rolled her eyes. "Selfish bastard."

Sam had no clue what to say. He offered her another cookie. She accepted it. Then she said, "The thing with people dying, it's like we're supposed to take those final hours, those final words, so damn serious. Like they've suddenly seen the truth and so we have to just accept it, just because we're the ones who've got to keep living and they're on their way out. I think that's horseshit. They don't know anything special. They haven't seen any light, yet. What they say ain't worth any more." She reached into her mouth to pick at a molar. "You know what I mean?"

"Yes."

✦ ✦ ✦

On the day their mother died, Wendy had gone in to check on her because their father was still working out in the barn, and it was high time that their mother be offered lunch even though their father would have ordinarily been the one to do so. The rest of the children were crowded around the radio in the kitchen, listening to the baseball game. When Wendy returned from the bedroom, she got Sam's attention and gestured at him to follow, without making any fuss. The others did not notice when the two eldest disappeared into their parents' bedroom. Wendy closed the door behind them.

His mother was dead, Sam knew this in an instant. He felt it in the air, as distinct as a sudden and extreme change of temperature or barometric pressure: there was not a third soul in this room.

She lay on her back, arms at her sides. Her eyes and mouth were slightly opened, but the expression on her face was not appalled, nor appalling. There was no blood. No vomit. No stench. There was no terror in this scene.

Wendy whispered, "Will you stay here while I get Dad? I don't want any of the others to come in and see her this way."

Sam nodded, and Wendy left the room behind him.

Sam gazed at his mother's bedside table, where there was an empty water glass, a pair of reading glasses, a book, a notepad and pen; all things that were always there. Then he approached, feeling foggy and faint, like the attachment of his head to his body was straining to come loose. When he reached the table, his eyes fell to the notepad, where his mother sometimes wrote requests instead of voicing them: *Less salt*, or *More tablets by Tuesday*. Now Sam's eyes swam over the words on the top page, dated today, in his mother's handwriting, which had grown very shaky and sloped over the years. It was almost a full page long. It began: *Jim—In spite of everything, and this, please know how much I have loved you, and the children.*

Sam did not read beyond this point, but he did read these words a second time, then a third, and he felt a thick muscular snake climbing up his throat. He felt a most vulgar rage. He felt betrayed. Lied to. For a moment, he felt this so intensely that he wished his mother was alive so that he could kill her again, himself; so offensive was her cowardice, so insulting were her lies.

Swiftly and without any consideration, Sam ripped the page from the top of the notepad, to expose an old note from a previous day. He crumpled the letter and put it in his pocket and later that day, he threw it in the fire without even reading the whole thing. At the time it didn't matter to him what she said, beyond those first words. She opened with lies, so there was no reason to expect there was truth anywhere on that page.

Fortunately, Wendy had not seen the note, Sam didn't believe; he hadn't gotten the impression she had approached the body before coming to retrieve him. Or even if Wendy had seen it, it occurred to Sam, she wouldn't have been able to read it, as Wendy did not read. So Wendy would not have to know. No one else would ever have to know. No one else would have to be told that it was possible for someone who loved you to live and die this way. They were all better off, he thought, never knowing that of all the words to say in her dying moments, their mother had chosen to lie.

It was the one time in his whole life that Sam had acted on impulse. Totally unlike himself. And every day since, he had regretted it, aware now that he had not only denied himself the knowledge of her final words, but had stolen them from everyone else, too.

Would those words have changed any lives?

Wendy had initiated the theory that the overdose had been accidental, and Sam quickly fell in line, realizing that to suggest suicide might lead down a path that ended with him being forced to confess to his theft of the note. So he vocally supported Wendy's theory even as Jack and Maeve stubbornly insisted it was suicide, and still did to this day, as far as Sam knew.

Sam did not know what his father made of all this, but felt the most guilt on his account; the letter was addressed to Jim, after all. Sam had always been confounded by his father's devotion to his mother, which hinted at a deeper love and understanding between the two of them than the children could grasp, and so, Sam wondered, did his father know his wife well enough to be suspicious of the fact that there was no note? His father had never voiced doubts, but Sam didn't think that necessarily meant that he'd never had them. His father was ill now, probably nearing the end. He would die never knowing those words, possibly the most important words that had ever been directed to him in his entire life. Sam hated himself for this.

What were those words? Sam's mind returned to them most often in the night, when they took strange shape in his dreams; sometimes scrawled grotesquely in a book meant for children and distorted by cheery images, sometimes as a chorus sung in a foreign tongue, sometimes floating just out of his reach, in smoke that dissipated too quickly to read. He longed for those words, obsessed over them, convinced himself that they could be retrieved telepathically with enough concentration, convinced himself that they were one thing, then another thing, then a completely different thing.

When Sam replayed the moment in his head, his vengeful and impetuous decision to destroy the words, he could not fathom his certainty in that moment that he was doing the right thing. He understood now, of course, that there was little in this world that could ever be known. You could think and feel and reason all you wanted, but *knowing* was something entirely different. Knowing was chicanery, a fool's paradise.

Norma said, "You must've stood by some deathbeds, being in service and all, yeah? Privy to some last words yourself, yeah? I don't mean to be crude."

Sam nodded. "I was with a few men when they died."

"What sorts of things did they say? I'm curious."

Norma didn't have a clue how she came off, it was why she ate lunch alone.

Sam didn't have to think hard at all to remember what his dying comrades had said in their last moments because every single one of them had expressed the same thing with their final breaths. Did that make it a truth? Or, as Norma seemed to think, did being close to death simply give a sentiment the weight and the illusion of truth when in fact it was every bit as obscured in those moments as any other—or perhaps even more?

Either way, he saw no reason not to answer Norma's question honestly. He said, "They all cried for their mothers."

Tito

1903

Nowadays Jim Shaw was forbidden from naming the farm animals, who were for milk and meat only. He'd gotten too attached in the past, hoped for too much. He still gave them names in his head, though, and made a mistake one day at lunch when his mother asked how he'd spent his morning and he said, "Tito got his neck caught in the barbed-wire fence."

"Tito?" his mother said.

Jim realized his mistake. "The neighbor boy," he said.

"We have a neighbor boy named Tito?" she said. "And he caught his neck in our fence?"

Jim nodded. His mother asked some more questions about Tito, like his age and where he lived, and Jim was forced to come up with quick lies. In truth, the only neighbors in walking distance of their home were Miss Harriet, the odd lady who lived alone in the tiny bungalow home, and the Bennington family, whose children were much older than Jim.

That evening when Jim and his father came in and washed up for supper, his mother said, "Guess who stopped by for a visit this afternoon? Tito's mother."

Jim stared at her.

She said, "She was so grateful you helped her son out of our fence this morning that she wanted to invite you to supper. I told her you'd walk over around five." She pointed toward the clock. "So you'd better head that way now. She said she'd send you home with a full belly in a few hours."

It took Jim a moment to process this. Oh, okay, his mother was lying in order to get him to confess to his lie. Well, he wasn't going to cave that easy. He could play this mean game, too.

Jim left the house. He walked up the drive with heavy feet, kicking at the dust and cursing and trying to decide where he was going to go for the next few hours to keep up this silly ruse. This was all Tito's fault. If he wasn't such a dumb goat, getting his neck stuck and all, none of this would have happened and Jim would be eating supper now. The last time Jim could remember being this upset was a few months ago, when his parents sent him to school. Although he was shy, he was excited at the prospect of making some friends, especially because he didn't have any brothers or sisters. His parents were trying, but as far as he could tell, that just kept not working out. Anyway, school hadn't worked out either.

Jim walked for a long while, all the way past Miss Harriet's bungalow, then got tired. He was hungry. He lay down in a ditch so he wouldn't be visible to passersby. He lay there so angry at Tito he eventually wore himself out, and fell asleep.

When he woke it was dusk, and the air was cool and alive with insects. He got up, brushed dried grass from his clothing, and headed home.

His mother was at the table. She said, "Where on earth were you?"

Jim said, "Tito's mother made dessert, too, vanilla ice cream on the back porch. We were having so much fun, they invited me to spend the whole night there. Tito begged, but I said I'd better be getting on home, with a full day of work tomorrow. Oh, we played some checkers, too, Tito and me. We had all sorts of fun."

His parents looked at each other.

Jim could see on the counter that there was leftover pie, but he wasn't going to touch it. He wasn't about to confess to his hunger and his lies.

His mother had a twinkle in her eye when she said, "Perhaps you'd like to have dinner there again tomorrow. I'm sure we can make arrangements."

Jim couldn't believe it, but he was suddenly crying. He felt betrayed by his own emotions, which were always conspiring to make him seem like such a different boy than he actually was.

His mother said, "Come here," and she held her arms open wide.

He sat on her lap and wept and came up with the only lie he could think of in that moment to explain his tears, "They were *mean*, Mommy, I wanted it to be fun, to have a friend, but Tito just kept laughing at how red my face got every time I had to talk. He wouldn't stop laughing."

Jim had told more lies today than in his entire life. He was usually cautious and honorable. But this had turned into such a mess and he couldn't seem to stop.

His mother rocked him and said, "I know. Shh, shh. I'm sorry. You don't have to go back. You will stay here at home, with me. This is where you belong."

The Bungalow

1911

Mrs. Ball was at her wits' end with her daughter, Marie, whose temperament had grown worse through adolescence. Now that Marie was sixteen and showed no signs of outgrowing the condition, Mrs. Ball was forced to consider the possibility that Marie would end up like her aunt Harriet (Mrs. Ball's sister), who suffered the same bizarre affliction: the moods, the misery, the need for silence and a dark room; a need that was presented as a life-or-death matter and could last days or even weeks. Harriet had not married, of course. What kind of man would tolerate a woman who frequently behaved like an invalid, though she suffered no physical ailment?

Harriet had left Baltimore in her early twenties and moved to rural Virginia on her own, buying herself a tiny one-room bungalow on a large plot of cheap land, where she had since lived in complete solitude and off the substantial inheritance the sisters had split. Mrs. Ball had only visited Harriet's bungalow once in the many years that she had lived there; Harriet had not been back to Baltimore a single time since moving away. The sisters exchanged letters from time to time, and Harriet had written recently to say that she was coughing up blood and unlikely to make it through the coming winter. She was not asking for a pity visit, she made clear.

Mrs. Ball's idea to send her daughter, Marie, to provide end-of-life care for Harriet was twofold. She thought the unsolicited offer of full-time live-in care would be received nicely by Harriet even if she claimed she didn't want the help. Also, Mrs. Ball thought, it could serve as a cautionary tale to Marie about ill-tempered women: what their life, and death, looked like. It was too late for her sister, but it wasn't too late for her daughter. Mrs. Ball had seen the pleasant side of her daughter often enough to know it existed, so she refused to accept that Marie's dark moods were a permanent feature or beyond her control, and thought that a bit of perspective might be just what Marie needed to get herself sorted out.

So that September, Mr. and Mrs. Ball arranged for Marie to travel by hired carriage from their home in Baltimore to the bungalow, where Marie was to provide aid to her aunt Harriet in her final months.

A few weeks later, Mrs. Ball received a letter from her daughter. Marie reported that upon her arrival she had learned that her aunt's illness was advanced and she was already relying on the kindness of neighbors to get by: the Benningtons brought bread twice a week and the Shaws sent their son, Jim, who was the same age as Marie, nearly every day with milk and produce, and to feed the hearth. Marie was embarrassed by the charity her aunt was accepting from these poor farming families, both of whom owned a fraction of the land that Harriet did, and Marie said she had promptly offered both families generous back pay for the help they had already provided Harriet, from the cash her parents had sent with her. The Benningtons accepted the money. The Shaws did not. Marie described Harriet's accelerated decline in the time she had been there: more blood in her sputum, less appetite, higher fever.

Then the tone of the letter took a turn, as Marie went on to write glowingly of country life; the beauty of the sprawling golden fields, the nobility of the blue mountain ridge in the distance, long solitary walks outdoors on paths well-trodden by Harriet through spindly orchards that smelled boozy-sweet, and by a pond where black-headed geese honked out tenor melodies in the evenings. She especially enjoyed working in Harriet's flower garden, where Harriet had instructed Marie on how to prepare for the first big frost: trim back the phlox, goldenrod, and other perennials, remove diseased plants, rake fallen leaves and arrange them around the plants to keep the soil moist and protected from the cold. Marie said that she appreciated the quiet consistency of her days. She even said she loved Harriet's bungalow, which Mrs. Ball had found so dismal on her visit many years earlier, small as it was and surrounded by towering maples that allowed for so little light indoors.

At the end of her letter, most distressingly, Marie inquired about family plans for Harriet's estate, explaining that she had not felt comfortable bringing this up with Harriet in her poor condition, but if Harriet's house was to remain in the family, she'd quite like to continue living there by herself after Harriet had passed. She pointed out that the garden would need lots of tending to in the spring; she hated to think of it languishing.

Mrs. Ball set the letter down, stunned to realize how profoundly her plan had backfired. She read it a second time, then took it to her husband's study and shared it with him. She told him that she and Harriet had never discussed the future of the estate, but Mrs. Ball assumed she would be the recipient, either through a will or implicitly as next of kin, because to the best of her knowledge Harriet had lived a completely solitary existence. She added that she didn't think it could possibly command much on the market, given its remote location and the small size of the home; unlivable, really, for more than a single occupant. Mr. Ball's stocks were doing very well and they certainly didn't need the money from Harriet's estate, but together they decided that, assuming it was left to the family, it ought to be sold promptly if for no other reason than to put the idea of staying there out of Marie's mind.

✦ ✦ ✦

Harriet passed away in January, and Mrs. Ball traveled to her home to retrieve Marie, empty the bungalow, and oversee the sale of the estate. (Mr. Ball could not take time away from work to join her.)

As she neared Harriet's bungalow, Mrs. Ball gazed out across the country that her daughter had written of with such fondness. Snow dusted the land in patches. There were wooded areas and large swaths of emptiness; some of the land flat, some of it thickly textured with slopes and summits. A distant blue ridge. All of this in the same view, as though whoever had designed it couldn't make up their mind. It was interesting enough, Mrs. Ball thought, if not beautiful.

Marie met her at the door of the bungalow and Mrs. Ball was instantly struck by how different her daughter looked. Marie's large eyes were bright. She greeted her mother warmly. Inside, Mrs. Ball could tell from the aroma of oil soap that Marie had been cleaning. There was an unusual arrangement of dried flowers on the table; lavender stems and pussy willow and lunaria and some other things Mrs. Ball had never seen before.

She said, "Did you make that? It's very pretty."

Marie nodded. Mrs. Ball noticed that Marie's hair had a nice sheen to it, and was styled in an intricate knot. She could see at the hearth that something was cooking.

Marie said, "I've made a chicken cream stew."

Mrs. Ball was touched by the preparations her daughter had made for her arrival, and she thrilled at the idea that she was going to be bringing home a different Marie; one who was finally taking an interest in her appearance and domestic duties, and, hopefully, had finally developed some appreciation for her mother.

But her good cheer was short-lived. Because once she was settled, she asked Marie where Harriet's paperwork, and presumably her will (if there was one) could be found, and Marie informed her mother gently that the estate had already been handled.

Mrs. Ball frowned. Before she could inquire further, Marie went to the desk and produced Harriet's will, which left her estate not to her next of kin but to her neighbors, the Shaws and the Benningtons.

After handing it to her mother, Marie took a few steps away from her before adding, "A lawyer's already been out to oversee the details and division of the property, so the land can be cleared and tilled and ready for plant by this spring. All of this happened weeks ago, when Harriet was still alert enough to facilitate it."

Mrs. Ball gawked at her daughter. "And you didn't think to notify your parents?"

"Harriet didn't want me to. She thought you might object and try to intervene."

"Well! Well! I only object to the secrecy. It's not like we need the money. This is a surprise and I don't like that part of it." Mrs. Ball sniffed, feeling betrayed by both her sister and her daughter, thinking she might have to cry soon. She said again, with pride, "It's not about the money."

"I know," Marie said.

Mrs. Ball wiped her nose. "And these kindly neighbors saw no problem accepting such an extravagant gift? You don't suppose they were scheming for it all along, swooping in to help when they knew her health was failing?"

Marie shook her head vehemently. "Both families were shocked."

Mrs. Ball wanted to throw something or slap someone. She had slapped Marie before, but not recently of course. She had slapped Harriet, too, for that matter, when they were girls. She got so mad when people were indecent with her, or plain stupid.

"And as Harriet pointed out," Marie continued, "the land is worth way more to the neighbors than you. They can actually grow their current farming operations, tenfold."

"And this house?" Mrs. Ball said. She looked around the place. Four hundred square feet, furnished entirely with dark wood. Small windows of warped glass with splintering frames, stained rugs, and fraying curtains. It didn't even look like there was a lock on the door. Yes, Marie had done some cleaning, but you couldn't change the nature of a place with a little bit of polish.

Marie said, "The way they divided things, the Shaws ended up with this house, but it's not going to be livable for a while. When a lawyer and appraiser came out, they discovered how badly the roof's sagging here in the center"—she pointed above her head—"and there's so much water damage to the rafters the entire roof needs to be replaced before anyone could live here safely. They said we're lucky it hasn't already collapsed."

"What do these Shaws want a house like this for anyway? Haven't they got their own?"

"Yes, they have."

"So they want to level it? Or renovate? Oh, what do I care?" Mrs. Ball said bitterly. "I don't know why I even asked. It's their house now and I always hated it anyway." She flopped an angry hand through the air before her face. "Rotting roof." She straightened up, tightened her collar. There was no reason to drag this out. Maybe she wouldn't need to cry after all. "No point in us sticking around if everything's been handled. We'll just clear your things out. Let's be ready to leave first thing in the morning."

Marie didn't move or speak for a moment, then she said, "The Shaws said that I'm welcome to stay in the house if I want, as long as I want."

Mrs. Ball felt a lurching twist in her belly.

Marie continued: "They know how much I love it here. And the way they see it, it's nothing to them to think of me remaining in the house, in light of the land they're getting. They said it's the least they could offer our family, considering."

"And the—but the—well, you said, the roof?" This was the least significant of Mrs. Ball's questions but the only one that she could think to address at this very moment.

"While the roof is being repaired here," Marie explained, "I will stay in their farmhouse. With their family. It's just Jim and his parents, and we're all friendly."

So the conspiracy went even deeper, Mrs. Ball realized, the

deception even further. "Of course they have a son. And I assume he's marrying age?"

"Well . . ." Marie caught her lip under her teeth before confessing, "Yes. But—"

"It's all so convenient, every bit of it!" Mrs. Ball howled. Now she understood: The nicely styled hair was not for her. Chicken cream stew. Cleaning. Of course none of it was for her.

Marie said, "There's no plan like that."

Mrs. Ball knew better, of course. "It's all decided then," she nearly spat, a nasty chill zipping through her. "You're not coming back to Baltimore. You're throwing away every opportunity your father and I ever gave you, to become one of these—these—these *Shaw* people."

"Jim and I are only friends. And I told you I wanted to stay here before I knew the Shaws at all," Marie reminded her mother. "It's calm here. And the way Harriet lived, never having to explain herself to anyone, and—"

"Oh goddamn Harriet. Forget Harriet. She was a miserable wretch, in case you failed to notice that. And in case you failed to notice that her niece from Baltimore had to travel all this way to help her in her final months, because she didn't have anyone else who cared enough—"

"The neighbors—"

"Goddamn the neighbors, too, those schemers, the crooks." Mrs. Ball was seething. "Don't you see how selfish you're being, picking them over me? How thankless, after everything I've done for you? The way I've looked after you, so patient, waiting for you to outgrow this thing? I've done plenty more than most mothers would, coddling you like an infant every time you refused to leave your bed . . ."

When this failed to provoke a reaction from Marie, Mrs. Ball got meaner, her daughter's rejection a sharp screw in her gut that just kept turning, and hurting worse with every rotation. *To hell with the land and the house. To hell with Harriet and the Shaws.* Mrs. Ball was so aggrieved that she could scarcely breathe. Her eyes were heated by tears, and the blade of her tongue grew even sharper. "I don't suppose these saintly Shaws have seen that side of you, have they?" she said. "They love the idea of you living in their home now, marrying their son, but just wait until they've seen . . . see . . ." Mrs. Ball felt her face flush incandescently, thinking about the sacrifices she had made, and now, the dashed hopes. "See, your own mother *has* to love you. Your own family haven't got a choice. I don't know if someone like you can possibly understand what a burden . . . But outside of your own flesh and blood . . . You just wait and see how these people feel about you once they actually know you."

Instantly, Mrs. Ball felt remorse for these words. She couldn't look at her daughter. She knew she could be terrible when she was hurt. It would have been better to just give Marie a smack, she thought, to dispense with the worst of her anger that way. She said simply, "I'm sorry."

When Marie replied it was not with anger but a tremulous

mix of hope and fear: "I think I might be better. I haven't had one of my spells since I got here."

Mrs. Ball turned away from her daughter and went to the window. The sky was dark now, a cavernous, yawning black that one could not find in the city.

She knew that Marie was wrong, despite her healthy appearance and efforts at an improved lifestyle. Because for as many times as Mrs. Ball had tried to convince herself in the past that her daughter was finally better, that she'd suffered her last spell, that the possibility of a fine life for Marie was still possible, she had always known in her deepest self where truths cowered that it was not so; it would never end. Furthermore, Mrs. Ball knew from experience that the more time passed between her daughter's spells, the worse the next one would be. So if it was true that it had been five months since the last, Mrs. Ball thought, then God only knew what the next one would look like. The darkness always caught up and settled the score.

But there was no point in trying to convince Marie of this now. Her mind was made up. Her hopes were high. So Mrs. Ball gathered herself, apologized to her daughter again for her harsh words, and offered some halfhearted ones of support. Mrs. Ball had no more fight in her. And it was apparent that Marie wasn't looking for a fight anyway, because she accepted her mother's apology with the ease of someone who had never expected any better, and didn't even care enough to bother with a grudge. It was time for Mrs. Ball to accept her daughter's decision, and go home.

✦ ✦ ✦

Mrs. Ball left early the next morning, when the sky to the east was a strip of golden, glimmering honey but the sun had not yet met the horizon. The air smelled metallic, of cold, and faintly of woodsmoke. It was very still. If there were birds around there, they weren't singers. Despite her shock at what had transpired there, and grief at the likelihood that she would see little more of her daughter in the coming decades than she had of her sister, Harriet, in adulthood, Mrs. Ball also felt a morsel of relief. She was eager to be home in Baltimore again, where the streets teemed with possibility and smiling faces.

A little way down the road, Mrs. Ball saw a tall young man heading in the direction of Harriet's bungalow on foot, carrying a wire basket. The Shaw boy, she thought, whom her daughter was sure to marry despite Marie's insistence that they were only friends. From this distance she could make out only an ample nose, dark hair, broad shoulders on an otherwise lanky frame. She had a thought to introduce herself to him, but decided against it. She didn't know what he might have heard about her from Harriet or Marie, and she hated conversations that she couldn't predict.

Mrs. Ball hunkered low in the carriage until she had passed him, and only turned back for a second look when she was a good distance down the road. As she stared at the glass bottles jostling in his wire basket, she felt some ill will, but also, mostly, pity, for this poor, naive young man who had no idea what sort of a life awaited him.

Marie did not end up moving into the bungalow, because—Mrs. Ball was correct on this point—before the roof was repaired, she and Jim had fallen in love and declared their intention to marry. By this time, it had been over a year since Marie's last dark spell, back in Baltimore, and a year was by far the longest she had ever in her life gone between spells, so Marie was convinced she was cured; that the country, the quiet, and the love of a good man had driven the darkness out of her.

The Shaw family farmhouse was large enough that Marie, Jim, and his parents were comfortable continuing to cohabit, and so when the bungalow was fit for an occupant, Marie was the one who suggested selling it on its own small plot and using the profit to purchase the Hereford cattle that would occupy the western pasture.

Jim said, "Are you sure we oughtn't keep the bungalow? For sentimental reasons? Or any other reasons?"

Marie thought for a bit then said, "No, we should get rid of it."

The bungalow was purchased by a man whose wife had thrown him out of their home on account of his drinking. The Shaws saw little of him, though he was friendly enough, and he surprised them by faithfully tending Harriet's garden, as well as Marie or Harriet herself would have done; it thrived under his care.

Marie became pregnant with her and Jim's first child, Wendy, the following year. It was during this pregnancy, around Christmastime, that Marie experienced her first dark spell since leaving Baltimore. It crashed into her like a black train, it sucked every good thought and good feeling out of her in an instant. She did her best to explain to Jim. She said she had allowed herself to hope that the darkness was behind her, but that had been foolish. She warned him that she was now convinced she would only be able to endure a certain number of dark spells in her life; she just didn't know what that number was.

Jim had always been a quiet individual, and throughout his life people would assume this was because he didn't put much stock in words. But it was the opposite; Jim spoke little because he held words in such high esteem. Words scared him because he recognized the gravity, the substance, the force of each one. So when he fell silent it was merely because he wanted to mean precisely what he said next.

But he thought and thought and still couldn't land on anything quite right to say to his wife, so he reached for her hands instead, and the interlacing of their fingers was somehow like a past meeting a future for the first time. And although there was nothing remotely reassuring about this moment, they would both remember it for the rest of their lives, that feeling of twenty trembling fingers gathered together like a nest.

✦ ✦ ✦

The man in the bungalow drank himself to death that same winter. He had not written a will, so the bungalow went to his wife, to whom he was still legally married though they hadn't seen each other in years. She had no interest in the place, nor any urgent need for the money, so it sat unoccupied for a while until eventually the wife contacted an estate agent about putting it on the market, and when the two of them met at the bungalow to discuss the sale she explained the circumstances of her husband's having lived there and she looked around the place with distaste, and she said, under her breath, "Can you believe he thought this place was the answer?" And the estate agent thought to himself, *How do you know it wasn't?*

The End

1955

Jim Shaw wanted to die at home, so Wendy learned how to administer all his medications. When the time drew near, Jim asked Wendy to call all her siblings to let them know it would probably happen soon, and that he didn't expect them to travel, he just didn't want the news to come as a surprise to anyone. Wendy suggested that Jim make these phone calls himself. She said she thought they'd like to hear his voice, even though their family had never been much for talking on the phone, and Jim in particular had never been much for talking at all. "Are you sure?" he asked, in earnest.

Jim was exhausted by the time he finished the sixth and final call—he told Wendy he'd probably nap all the way until dinner. He was embarrassed by his children's tears and expressions of love. He'd done all right by them, he supposed, though there had been plenty of failures and regrets, two in particular that had never stopped hurting.

The first: that he had not been the one to find his wife. Marie's death was painful but not a surprise; early on in their marriage Jim had been forced to accept the likelihood that the darkness would win. Still, he did everything he could over the years to support Marie's efforts to manage and survive the thing. He accepted all sorts of bizarre distortions of her personality, and inexplicable behaviors brought on by medication and other unsuccessful treatments and the darkness itself. He never stopped defending her to the children as one by one they lost patience and respect for her. In Marie's final years she was so diminished by it all, the toll taken on her brain and body and spirit by the failed efforts and the dashed hopes, that Jim didn't argue against increased dosages of her sleep medications. He watched as each day she spent fewer and fewer minutes awake, and he knew when the line between her life and her death had become so thin that it would not take much at all to officially cross it. When she started skipping and stockpiling medication, he pretended not to notice, even though his heart was broken.

He didn't know why she chose that exact day, but he knew why she chose that exact time of day: to spare any of the children the added trauma of finding her. Jim was always the one to bring her lunch. The children never entered her room unannounced in the afternoon. But that day, Jim was distracted by the task of shoeing the mare, he was enjoying his quiet work and the company of the animal so immensely that he lost track of time and was late coming in. Had he been on time, he would have been the first to find Marie. As it happened, instead, Wendy thought she'd better check on her mother instead of waiting for Jim. Later, when

Wendy offered the opinion that the death was likely accidental, of course Jim knew better, and thought surely Wendy did, too. But when he saw how the youngest children, Henry and Bette, seemed to find comfort in the idea that it was a mistake, he didn't see any reason to dispel it.

To this day, though, Jim couldn't forgive himself for the fact that it was Wendy who found the body and not him. Furthermore, unbelievably, Jim had been whistling when Wendy came to tell him. How could that be, the whistling? Wasn't the world supposed to give you signs? Oughtn't there have been a chill in the air when his wife drew her last breath? Oughtn't he have felt some terrible stirring in his soul, a shift in his reality? Oughtn't time have stood still? But there was nothing; up until the moment Jim was told, he was as dumb and happy as the animal he was tending.

This was Jim's only true regret when it came to his wife. He knew others might wonder about the very basis of their union, if he regretted marrying such a troubled woman. Marie remarked on this herself during dark times: how difficult she was to love, how impossible. She insisted he must feel regret for having married her. On the day they were married, Jim had promised Marie: *I will always be faithful to you.* He realized later that he had committed to faith in her, and in their union, without knowing remotely what type of faith, and how much, would be required of him. Still, even at their worst times, Jim did not experience the pain as regret. The love he had for her, the faith he maintained, was a mountain. It was astonishing in its magnitude, and hard, and imposing, and mysterious. Even when it was inextricable from suffering, one did not feel *regret* for such a thing.

The handling of his daughter Lane's early pregnancy was Jim's second great regret in life. Jim had maintained his own dark suspicions about John Winthrop and the pregnancy. He had urges to confront the young man when the news was announced, urges that advanced to fully realized thoughts of murder. He lay awake devising plans, he considered logistics for the farm and the family should he spend the rest of his life in prison. But Lane had gone to such great and unfailing lengths to dismiss all negative notions about John Winthrop, and to express her desire to raise the child with him, that Jim realized in his efforts to defend his daughter he was both accusing her of a lie, and denying her the life she wanted to live.

Lane never relented on her story, so Jim accepted it. But he never shook John Winthrop's hand. Not on the day their marriage was made official, not following the birth of the child. When he learned of his son-in-law's death in service, Jim had to fight the temptation to ask for details, such as the extent to which John Winthrop had suffered. He never stopped feeling that he should have done more, or less, to try to reach the truth, for Lane.

✦　✦　✦

Mercifully though, now as the end drew near, Jim's regrets, the two big ones and countless small others, seemed to lose their claws, appearing only briefly and as dull and curious aches, no longer as barbs or in spasms. Mostly, these days, Jim's thoughts were of his children when they were small, the burbling roll of their laughter, the thumping of their bare heels across the hardwood, dirt and grease and milk and tears and jam on bright faces. The most unremarkable moments were now so precious in his memory, infused with such sweetness and radiant light, that they sent tremors through Jim.

A warm summer breeze curled through Jim's bedroom and carried with it the aroma of the towering juniper just outside his window. He could faintly hear a goldfinch trilling. Wendy was hanging laundry, otherwise he'd have called to her and asked her to crack the window a little wider so he could have even more of this pleasure. But who did he think he was, demanding this pleasure? He was not a special man! He had not lived a special life! And yet there it was again, that breeze and that smell and that song, and Jim felt something in his heart that he'd not felt before: a most fierce joy, a staggering gratitude. It woke him all the way up. It expelled all the questions, as though it were the most singular and final and obvious answer. Although it was so powerful it almost felt like violence, there was no pain in it. No pain. Just joy. He waited for this joy to pass, or to diminish. It did not.

Advent

1959

Many things had changed for the family in the years since Jim Shaw's funeral. Bette and her two young daughters, Lane and her teenage son, and Jack, had all moved into the Shaw family farmhouse within a year of Mr. Shaw's passing.

These actions were decided over the course of Jim's funeral weekend, when it became apparent that Bette and Lane, both widowed, and Jack, divorced, newly sober, but not employed—were all struggling in their current circumstances. Another factor was the information provided by a Realtor: the Shaw property, which had already been sold off but for two acres, was worth more for the remaining acreage than the home itself, and the house would almost certainly be demolished if the property sold. Lastly, and although she wouldn't say so herself, it was clear to the others that Wendy was at a loss for where she would go and what she would do with herself if the house were sold. The other siblings—Sam, Maeve, and Henry—all dismissed talk of a split or a buyout where the house was concerned; none of them needed money and all were happier with the idea of the home staying in the family. And so, a course of action was happily agreed upon.

Bette had inherited a great deal of money when her husband passed, and she put some of this toward an addition and remodel of the Shaw house that added over a thousand square feet to the home, to accommodate all its new residents.

Now, years later, Wendy, Jack, Lane, and Bette had finally managed to convince the rest of the siblings to bring their families for a big Christmas in the Shaw family home. "Just like old times!" they said with varying measures of enthusiasm, though of course it would bear no resemblance to old times. Now, the children were in their thirties and forties. Now, they were the parents, they were veterans and workers and widows, now the world had tossed them about and dented them into all sorts of new shapes.

Those who were traveling made their arrangements, and those who lived at the family home started readying it several weeks in advance of Christmas.

The bad news of the holiday season did not come as a surprise, but it was still a crushing blow: Lane's son, Thomas, would not be home for Christmas. Lane learned this not from Thomas himself, but through a letter sent on Thomas's behalf, from Del, the leader of the commune where Thomas lived. It was obvious that this letter was not personal to Lane, but had been photocopied and sent to many mothers to inform them that their children would not be home for the holidays and there was no need to bother trying to convince them, nor contact them at all. Gifts would not be accepted. Phone calls would not be returned. Christmas was not recognized by this group that Thomas was now a part of.

Thomas had dropped out of college this past spring to move to the commune. He had been persuaded by a musician who traveled through his college town and played a show at a local bar. Thomas and several other students in attendance ended up conversing with the musician late into after-hours, drugs were almost certainly involved, and by the end of the night, the musician had convinced five students to leave everything behind—their belongings, education, and family ties—to go live on a compound in central Tennessee. It was a few weeks before Lane had learned of this, the news first coming from the provost's office at Thomas's college, informing her that Thomas had not been attending class and was being administratively withdrawn. Tuition would not be refunded.

It didn't take long for campus security to figure out where Thomas had gone, because he had communicated his intentions to his roommate. The roommate couldn't remember the name of the musician who had convinced Thomas and the others to join him, but he knew they were headed to Tennessee, near some wildlife-management area with a funny name. A few quick calls to the authorities in Cumberland County, Tennessee, confirmed the existence of a commune located just outside Catoosa, that had claimed a number of new residents in the past few months. Their local office had fielded phone calls from other desperate parents, like Lane. But provided the individual was over eighteen years old, there was nothing the authorities could do to intervene.

Lane was, however, provided a number for a phone line that was believed to be located on the commune. She called this number, and the girl who answered the phone sounded very young and very sleepy. Lane begged. Eventually, the girl agreed to track down Thomas. She was away from the phone for several minutes.

Lane wept when she heard her son's voice.

Thomas's voice was odd though, it was strident and cold when he explained to her that he had chosen a different life path, he was committed to this spiritual journey, and Lane wouldn't need to understand, but she would need to accept it.

She said, "I'm coming for you."

He said, "Don't. I'm not leaving. It will be a waste of your time."

Lane struggled to contain a sob that wrenched her back. "Can I come visit you at least? Not to bring you home or try to change your mind. Just to see your face."

It was quiet for a moment, long enough that her hopes spiked, but then Thomas said, "No. Not now. Maybe one day, but not now."

Lane said, "Do they feed you?"

"We grow our own food. There's more than enough to go

around and we don't have to drive some gas-guzzling vehicle to a capitalist establishment to buy chemically poisoned food out of a can. We get everything we need straight from the earth." He paused, then said, "I do have to go now though."

"Wait," Lane said. She had the sensation of drowning, arms in the air, water in the lungs. "What do you need? What can I do?"

"I'm fine," Thomas said. "Please don't call again. It's a hassle for whoever answers to come track me down. And we aren't really into too much contact with the outside world, we're trying to maintain purity."

"How will I know you're okay?"

"I'll call you sometime to check in."

"When?"

"I don't know."

All of this had been many months ago. So Lane had had no reason whatsoever to believe that Thomas would actually come home for Christmas. But the fact that everyone else would be there—all her siblings, that is—was one miracle, and somehow she had foolishly hoped for a second one.

Lane showed Jack the Christmas letter from the commune as soon as she received it, which was on a Saturday, a week before Christmas.

Jack was incensed. He and Thomas had become close in the past few years, since living together at the Shaw family house.

They found the same sorts of things interesting and funny, and enjoyed smoking cigarettes together on the porch late into the night. They shared a strong family resemblance; Thomas looked more like his uncle Jack than he did his own mother, or his deceased father. And when Jack had accompanied Lane to move Thomas into his dormitory, he'd even shed a few tears, like a father might, as they drove away from campus. Jack had taken the initial news of Thomas's move to the commune very hard.

"Morons!" Jack spat now, after reading the Christmas letter. He tossed the paper onto the table, went to the kitchen window, and stared outside for a minute, fists working, then spun around and said, "This nonsense has gone on long enough. We're going to get him."

Lane stared at her brother. "Really?"

"It's time we get the kid out of there. Enough's enough."

"He's a grown man," Lane said. "We can't force him. He's been very clear on me not coming."

"He needs some sense talked into him is all," Jack said. "We'll leave now, be back by tomorrow evening. I'll get the atlas."

Lane left a note for Wendy and Bette, who were at the store with Bette's daughters. Then Lane and Jack packed things for one night in a hotel.

The gray sky churned like it was working up something terrible, but it didn't begin to snow until they reached Christiansburg.

It started with little crystalline flakes that doinked off the windshield, then turned to fluffy wet clusters that quickly accumulated to slush on the road, slowing the pace of traffic.

They crossed the border into Tennessee and stopped for gas and an early dinner at a White Castle.

After eating, Jack got out the atlas to double-check their route. The snow was growing heavier by the hour.

Lane said, "Think we'll make it before dark?"

Jack gestured out the window. "Not in this. I think our best bet's to make as much headway as we can, stay in a hotel near the compound, and go there first thing in the morning. Catch him when he's fresh out of bed."

On they went, through snowfall and into darkness.

They reached Cumberland County by eight o'clock, and checked into a two-queen room at the Howard Johnson's. By their best estimate, they were about fifteen miles from the compound, which was said to be located on the eastern border of the Catoosa wildlife area. Jack bought some Hostess snacks from the lobby, but Lane was not hungry. She had a sickly dreadful feeling. She actually wanted a drink, quite badly. Jack didn't mind them having alcohol around the house—he'd insisted way back when they were all moving in that there not be a moratorium on account of his sobriety—but Lane hadn't thought to pack anything for herself and wasn't about to go out for something.

Jack switched on the television and they watched an episode of *Maverick*. During a commercial break, he said, "I'm thinking we pull up, survey the scene, you stay in the car, I'll head into whatever sort of building seems like the main one, if somebody hasn't already approached us. I'm assuming they stay up all night and sleep till noon, so I'll be catching them when they're bleary and unprepared. Either way, you should just wait in the car and let me do the talking."

"You think that's the right approach?"

"Tone of that letter they sent," Jack said, "I think we're better off if I make it clear we mean business."

Lane got up, opened the curtain a few inches, and stared out into the night. Snowflakes swirled around the streetlamps. Since leaving home that afternoon, darkness had oozed about in Lane's organs, pressing outward. It was a concentrated version of the fear and despair she had felt since Thomas first left. There was hope in there, too, somewhere, it came in faint sparks, but it did not withstand reason; as soon as Lane applied a real thought to that hope, it dissipated.

Jack changed into his pajamas in the bathroom and crawled into his bed. "Aim to check out of here around seven?"

Lane nodded. "Jack, what are you going to say to him?"

"I'm gonna say, *Your mom's going to die of a broken heart if you're not home for Christmas. She'll die and the blood will be on your hands.* I'll make like we'll bring him back here after the holiday, like it's just about Christmas. Main thing is we've just got to get him away from that place and those people even if that entails some little white lies. Once he's out of their grip, I don't think it will be hard to convince him not to go back."

"What if he refuses to come with you?"

"He won't."

"What if other people there try to intervene? This Del person?"

"I'll let Del throw the first punch, start the fight, and I'll finish it."

"You won't. Promise you won't fight."

"No promises."

Jack snored loudly in the night. When Lane knocked off, her dreams were tortured and intense scenarios where she found herself powerless as disfigured faces taunted and pursued her.

The hazy brightening of the room with dawn and then the alarm shortly after came as a relief, and Lane rose swiftly to shower and ready herself to leave. Jack retrieved coffees from the lobby and two Danishes wrapped in plastic. The snow had let up in the night and although the grim sky looked ominously active, it was not snowing at present and vehicles appeared to be moving at a normal speed. Lane applied lipstick, then removed it.

In the car, she spread the atlas over her lap, and they headed west. The coldness and grayness of the air gave the claustrophobic impression of a heavy fog. They were on the highway for a short time, then took a winding exit toward Catoosa, and soon entered a heavily wooded area. They turned onto a narrow dirt road marked OTTER DRIVE. They passed a sign for DADDY'S CREEK, a sign for OBED RIVER. There was a crust of snow on the ground, and Jack adjusted his speed accordingly. Lane felt her racing heart distinctly in her temples and in her gut.

Jack slowed down as they approached what appeared to be a long driveway with dilapidated fencing on both sides. There was a mailbox, and he came to a full stop to see the number. This was it. He turned down the drive, which was difficult to navigate in the snow. Lane gripped her knees.

Soon the woods cleared, opening to what appeared to be a very old campground with five identical log cabins. Many of the windows were busted out and covered with plywood. There were no lights on within, though two of them had smoke rising from their chimneys. This smoke, and some footprints in the snow, were the only signs of life. There was some graffiti on the exterior of the cabins that Lane could not read. There was a bonfire site in the center of it all, with huge blackened logs and wooden benches surrounding it in a semicircle. There was one vehicle on the premises: a rusted mid-1940s Ford pickup with a crack spidering through its windshield.

Jack put the car in park and said, "We made it, Laney. Paradise." He surveyed the area for another minute, then said, "Reckon I'll start with that one," and pointed to the nearer cabin with a smoking chimney. "Leave the engine running, and climb into the driver's seat, why don't you, just in case we need to be speedy getting out of here."

Lane said, "You expect that?"

"No. I expect to walk out of that cabin calmly with Thomas

in no time. But just in case it's not so calm, we should be ready to skedaddle."

"You promised you weren't going to fight," Lane murmured, though she remembered now as she said this that in fact what Jack had actually said was, *No promises.*

"Look around," Jack said. "How hard can it possibly be to convince someone to leave this hellhole?"

Lane got out of the car, walked around it, and climbed into the driver's seat as Jack headed out over the snowy land with a confident, loping gait. He rubbed his hands together, then through his dark hair as he approached the cabin. His breath huffed out in clouds. Lane felt explosive, like the slightest startle could send her to the sky, in pieces.

She watched as Jack rapped on the door, then a few moments later, a second time.

He pressed his ear to the door as though he might have heard some action inside, and shortly, the door opened a crack. The angle was wrong for Lane to see who stood on the inside, but she could tell from Jack's response that the individual he was speaking to was taller than him.

Lane watched as Jack's posture grew obstinate, back on his heels, hands crossed over his chest. He took a step forward, toward the door, and a thick arm from inside extended to meet Jack's chest, not striking him but preventing his entry. Jack stood his ground. His voice became loud.

"Thomas." Jack was hollering, jimmying himself around to try to look inside, beyond the man in his way. "Thomas Winthrop? You in there?"

The hand from inside the door pushed out harder and farther, so that Lane caught a glimpse of the body it was attached to, a hulking, shadowy form, and then the hand met Jack's chest with force, sending him staggering several feet backward. The door slammed shut.

Jack got his balance and his bearings. Lane could see that his face had gone scarlet. He reached under his jacket and withdrew something.

Oh God, oh God, no. Lane's breath snagged, then stuck in her throat like a ball of thorns. *His service pistol.* Jack kept it at home in a safe in his bedroom. She'd never once known him to wield it and therefore didn't have strong feelings about its presence in their home one way or the other; she had practically forgotten the thing even existed. It hadn't occurred to her once that he might bring it along on this trip. He had hidden it, *she was deceived!*, this was not the plan!

Lane got out of the car and struck out through the snow in his direction shouting, "Jack, *no!*"

But before she had gotten anywhere near her brother, he had already reared back, met the door of the cabin with the heel of his foot, it splintered easily, and Jack busted in, firm grip on the pistol, which was aimed at the ground. Lane heard the yelling of men, more than two of them, and she stopped in her tracks. Was her son's voice part of this mix? She couldn't tell, she couldn't make out words. *No shots, please no shots*, she begged of the air, the men, God, the gun itself.

Suddenly, movement from the second cabin with a smoking chimney caught her eye, and a thin figure emerged from the front door of that cabin.

It was Thomas. Nearly nude, bearded, hair pulled back in a loose, low ponytail. He was pale, and skinny as spaghetti.

Lane shrieked, and though she found herself oddly unable to move toward him, she waved both hands in the air. She felt crushed by the weight of this moment, powerless against the forces and spirits at play. "Thomas!"

Thomas's gaze settled on her and he stared at his mother, panicked confusion stricken across his face, the way a small animal might stare at a predator who has laid an impressive trap.

Jack burst out of the first cabin at the sound of Lane's voice, the pistol still in his hand, and he followed her gaze to the porch of the other cabin where Thomas stood shivering in his underwear.

Jack lowered the pistol and shouted with exuberance, with hope, "Thomas! Come!"

Jack galloped toward his nephew, shoving the pistol back into its holster beneath his shirt, running with arms outstretched. Lane remained frozen, shocks of adrenaline jolting her.

As Jack approached Thomas, Thomas's shoulders gathered and he shrank in submission, like he expected to be struck. His chin dropped to his chest.

Jack slowed as he got near to Thomas and moved to embrace

the boy. But before he could, Thomas whipped up to full height and lurched forward like a snake to push Jack hard with both of his hands. Jack reeled back, teetering off the porch and into the snow. Lane finally found herself able to move, and she ran in their direction. Thomas stood on the porch, leering over Jack, wearing an expression Lane had never before seen on his face. It looked like hate.

Lane could see faces in the windows of Thomas's cabin, several faces at each window, most of them girls who looked very young. Lane had always looked young, especially when she was a teenager, so she found it hard to guess another woman's age, but these faces in the windows struck her distinctly as the faces not of women but of children.

The large man from the first cabin was approaching now, at a calm pace, and he carried a fire poker. His head was shaped like a block, his jaw the width of his temples. He pointed the fireplace poker at Jack and commanded, "Hands in the air."

Jack obeyed.

"Get off our land," the man growled, turning to Lane. "Both of you."

Lane gasped, "Thomas, Thomas," and Jack, who'd had the wind knocked out of him, wheezed, "Hell," but he kept his hands up, he did not reach for the handgun, to Lane's relief.

The large man bellowed, "*Now*."

Lane put her palms together and fell forward. Snow creaked

beneath her kneecaps. She said, to the large man, "Please let my son come home."

"He's free to do whatever he wants, always has been." He sneered, then turned to Thomas, who was now shivering violently and clutching his own elbows. The large man said, "You going or staying?"

Thomas looked at the large man, then at Jack, then at his mother, then back to the man. He said, "I'm staying, of course."

Lane began to weep. "No," she said.

In that terrible cold voice he had used on the phone with her, Thomas said, "How many times have I told you not to come, that it would be a waste of your time? Well, now you've gone and done it."

His nipples looked tiny and ridiculous in this cold. He was absurd to Lane, suddenly. A joke. A malnourished puppet. Where was her child? Who was this stranger and how was it that her love for him could swallow her whole, despite the fact that she scarcely even knew him?

Jack was rising to his feet, and the large man loomed over him. "Hands in the air," he warned again. "You go for the gun, I'll take your head clean off. You've trespassed on my land, threatened me and my people, and you're lucky you'll make it out alive."

Lane could see on Jack's face that it took every ounce of restraint not to reach for the gun, risking whatever violence this man was capable of in the split second it would take him to get at his own weapon. She could see in Jack's eyes the rage, the pride, the bloodthirst. Yet Jack managed to suppress the violence inside him, and he rose passively to his feet.

Lane made a final appeal to her son. She said, "Will you come sit in the car for five minutes, just to talk? Then we'll go."

Thomas sighed, with drama and disdain. "You didn't honor my request so I won't honor yours."

Jack came to his sister, the large man following closely behind him and slapping the fireplace poker menacingly into his palm. Jack knelt at Lane's side, then helped her to her feet. He brushed snow from her knees. He whispered gently, "Let's go. It's all right now. Time to go home."

He steadied Lane, holding her at the elbow, as they made their way back to the car.

Jack drove, and Lane cried, and then she was done crying, and they did not speak for a long while.

The snow had started back up again.

Eventually, Lane said, "What did you see in the first cabin?"

"Bunch of half-naked kids living like pigs. Garbage and mildew everywhere. Smelled like a barnyard."

"He's gonna come to his senses, isn't he? He's gonna come home."

Lane glanced at Jack, who glanced back but did not speak. Lane was expecting a more affirmative response from her brother. "You believe that, right?" she said. She reached over to grip his arm, panic returning and rising swiftly in her. "He will come home."

"Sure, yes," Jack said.

"You're the one that's been assuring me of that all along. What happened back there that I didn't see? What changed your mind? What do you know?" Lane demanded.

Jack patted her hand on his arm. "Nothing," he said. "I was just thinking."

"Thinking what?"

Jack stared at the road ahead. He turned the windshield wipers on and off. "I don't know if I should say."

"When have you ever in your life not said something on account of thinking you oughtn't?"

Jack was quiet for a little while. Eventually, he said, "When you got pregnant, I had half a mind to storm over to the Winthrop house with a gun."

Lane turned sharply to face him. "What?"

"And then when you left," Jack continued, "for good. When you moved to Chesterfield to raise Thomas with them. With *his* family. With *him*."

"John?"

Jack nodded. "I can't tell you how many times I thought about coming down there and bringing you back home. Waving a gun in their faces and saying, *She's ours! She belongs to us! She's coming home with me, now!*"

Lane blinked. "I had no idea you felt that way."

"I couldn't get it out of my head that he'd done you wrong," Jack said. "You were so young. I never got over the idea that I hadn't saved you from a bad situation and a bad guy. I'm sorry. I know you've said all you're ever going to say on it. But I hated his guts. I couldn't let it go. Not when you promised us it was okay back then, you promised that it had been . . . that you were . . . it was . . . consenting. Not when all the rest of them decided to take your word and told me I had to let it go, because that's what you wanted. Not when you raised Thomas with him, stuck by him all those years, not even when he died, or in all these years since. I never stopped thinking he'd done you wrong and I should've saved you. Never stopped being angry."

Lane's mouth was a dry hole. Her breath came in short and hot.

Jack looked at her. "Sorry," he said. "None of my business, is it? I know I should've just accepted him and let it go, like everybody else did."

Lane only learned that she was crying when tears dripped off her chin and splashed to her collarbone. Finally, finally. She experienced this word *finally*, not like a word but like a brand-new body rising up through her tired flesh. She felt what felt like the brightness of the whole white sun on her face.

"I told him no," she said. "Again and again. I tried to push him off but he was so much bigger. In the end . . . I guess I was just too shy to raise my voice."

She watched as Jack's face broke. "Oh, Laney," he said.

Lane wiped her face with her sleeve. "And once it was over, everything just started spinning forward. Life, I mean. With the pregnancy and all." She cycled her index fingers around one another. "It just went and went and went, life did, like a ball rolling down a hill, picking up speed, bouncing and spinning forward. You can't keep up. You can't stop. So once things settle and that ball comes to rest, I think your brain finds a way to make what happened . . . acceptable to you. It finds a way to make your life livable."

"I should have come for you," Jack said woefully. "I could've killed him, I wanted to."

"I wouldn't have let you," Lane said, "and if you'd come down trying to rescue me, waving a gun in John's face, I wouldn't have come home with you. My mind was made up."

Lane's thoughts turned to Thomas and the large man with the fireplace poker and the girls in the windows and her child's bare white legs, and the hatred in her child's voice and on his face, and she realized that maybe this was not actually hatred at all, but merely determination, sheer will, to keep believing the lie he was telling himself.

And this would pass, Lane thought, feeling suddenly and powerfully reassured by the notion. One can only maintain a lie, even to one's own self, for so long. The brain can only split itself into so many halves before the truth comes through, screaming like a banshee, shining bright as a flame, refusing to be silenced or ignored for one moment longer. The truth eventually makes its demands, she thought, and the children, even the most determined ones, eventually make their way home.

✦ ✦ ✦

Back at the Shaw house, when they returned from the grocery store with Bette's daughters, Wendy and Bette discovered Lane's note explaining her and Jack's whereabouts, as well as the Christmas letter issued by the commune. The two women passed both notes back and forth, exchanging looks but not wanting to discuss it in front of the girls, who knew nothing of the commune, or Del, or any of it. As far as they were aware, their eldest cousin, Thomas, was still just at college, and they didn't know enough to expect that he should've been home for summer, or now, for the holidays.

When they sat for lunch, Emma said, "Where is Uncle Jack? I thought we were going to work on the puzzle together this afternoon."

Bette said, "Him and Auntie Lane are away. They'll be back tomorrow."

"Where?" Emma demanded. "Why?"

Bette said, "Just a short trip. You don't need to know every detail."

"He said we would work on the puzzle," Emma pointed out.

Bette said, "I'll work on it with you," knowing full well that this would not satisfy Emma.

After lunch, Wendy got out the recipes for piecrusts. They would mix the dough up today and keep it in the freezer until Christmas Eve; one less thing to do when the whole family was in the house. She moved around Bette to retrieve the flour and the pastry blender. Bette reached for a mixing bowl. The two of them worked together in the kitchen often and had developed a strong unspoken working chemistry, moving easily to accommodate each other, anticipating needs and handing off measuring cups and sheet trays, passing rags for cleanup, in perfect synchrony.

Lane and Jack both worked full-time, Lane at the library and Jack at a tire-manufacturing plant, so Wendy and Bette did most of the homemaking. It had taken some time getting used to each other at first. They had barely spent any time together at all since Bette left home; a few funerals were the only occasions.

When Bette returned to move into the Shaw family home with her daughters, it was with deep shame. She was horrified by the way she had left all those years ago: thoughtless, thankless, egotistic, riding high on the money and status she was marrying into. Bette didn't discuss this shame with her siblings, and they mistook her guilt for grief over the death of their father. That grief was alive inside Bette, too, of course. And grief for her husband, Ray, who had passed several years prior. And worries for her daughters. Also, a lurking sadness that came and went and could not always be attributed to anything at all; it was a most capricious darkness. There were many shadows swirling inside Bette, known and unknown, tended to and neglected. It was maddening, Bette's brain, how it shape-shifted, how it gave and took from her life. But Wendy, who had spent more years with their mother than any of the rest of them, had a certain easy way with other people's darkness. She didn't resent it, take it personally, overanalyze, or internalize it. She seemed to just notice it, give a respectful nod in its direction, then go about her way.

Bette cut butter into chunks with a paring knife and said, "I can't believe these people, sending a letter like that to a mother, keeping her away from her child on Christmas. It's evil. Would you guess Jack or Lane will do the talking?"

"I'm sure Jack will insist," Wendy said, "although I imagine it would go smoother with Lane."

"Do you think they'll even set eyes on Thomas?" Bette said. "If they're trespassing, I don't imagine the law is on their side supposing they go stomping around the compound, making demands. What if Thomas refuses to see them?"

Wendy measured baking soda and sifted it into the other dry ingredients. "I don't know what, then," she said.

Wendy and Bette busied around with some more food preparation, then tidied up and did a quick sweep under the tree for stray needles. It was a Douglas fir that reached the ceiling, but the needles were a lot to keep up with. Several weeks earlier, the whole household had gone together to retrieve this tree: Wendy, Jack, Lane, Bette, and the girls. There was no squabbling about which tree to take home, all were in agreement as soon as they set eyes on this one. They strung colored bulbs around it, and many ornaments that the house had accumulated over the years, some crafted with pipe cleaners and Popsicle sticks, others elegant globes of etched glass. Wendy and Bette had collected boughs from the pines on their own property several days later and fashioned a large wreath with red ribbon and wire, for the front door. They wove some boughs and holly and ribbon around the mailbox, too. They put little battery-powered white candles in all the windows of the house. They wanted it to be as festive and inviting as possible for Henry and Sam and their families, and Maeve and her unconfirmed guest.

Jack and Lane returned to the house the next evening, with no Thomas.

Emma said, "We finished the puzzle without you."

Wendy said, "You must have run into snow." It had been falling throughout the day and there were several fresh inches on the ground.

After Bette had put her girls to bed, Lane told her sisters about the trip, though she left out the part about Jack's gun because she didn't want them giving him a hard time. She surprised herself by not crying, by feeling very little at all, actually, when she told them about Thomas's state. She described his appearance as rodent-like and his behavior as erratic. Unrecognizable to her, really. She did start to cry, though, when she told them about the faces of the young girls in the windows.

On the twenty-third of December, other members of the family started to roll in.

Henry, his wife, Anne, and daughter, Mimi, were the first to arrive. Mimi was very sassy and pretty, and Bette's daughters, Emma and Dawn, could not conceal their awe. Within minutes of their older cousin's arrival, Emma and Dawn went to their bedroom and returned with their hair back in barrettes, just like Mimi's was done.

Bette heated the kettle and offered hot buttered rum. Jack turned up the Bing Crosby Christmas album that was playing in the living room. Bette said to her daughters, "Why don't you show Mimi your room?"

On their way out of the kitchen, Emma said to her older cousin, "I bet you've got a boyfriend."

Wendy said to Henry's wife, Anne, "Why don't I show you the guest rooms and you decide which you want?"

Lane and Jack joined them, leaving Henry and Bette alone in the kitchen.

Henry looked around the room. "Renovations look great," he said.

"You think? I've been wishing I went with wallpaper in here. And darker cabinets."

"Anne loves this shade, it's what she's been wanting for ours."

"Are you planning a renovation?" Bette said.

"We need to decide if we're staying in the house before we go putting more money into it."

"You're thinking of leaving?"

"Just the house, not the neighborhood. We'd love a bigger yard. Anne loves gardening, you know."

"I didn't know."

"You should've seen everything she grew this past spring. Peas. Corn. Some flowers, too, I wouldn't know the names. She's amazing."

Bette stirred her hot buttered rum. It filled her with pleasure to be sitting there with Henry, listening to him brag about his wife. For so many stupid years, Bette had resented Henry for the happiness he had found outside their family. She could recall various occasions early in Henry and Anne's marriage when Bette had seethed over the way Henry's eyes darted nervously around the room when Anne left him alone with Bette; how desperate he was for his wife to return, how strongly he desired his wife's company. It had shocked Bette that it could cause her so much pain for her brother to fall in love, to prefer his wife to his sister. It wasn't like Bette had yearned to return to their childhood circumstances, but if she wasn't Henry's best friend, his favorite in this world, she didn't know how to be something else with him. This had borne such animus. But that had changed somewhere along the way, it had broken loose, and now it was so natural for Bette to feel uncomplicated goodwill toward Henry and Anne that it would have taken real effort to feel anything else.

Henry said, "How's it been with Thomas and all?"

"Lane told you?"

Henry nodded. "In the spring, when he first left. We spoke about it on the phone. Have they heard anything?"

"Lane and Jack drove out to the compound a few days ago. Saw him with their own eyes, which I suppose was reassuring in some sense, but he wasn't about to leave with them."

Henry said matter-of-factly, "He'll be back."

"You think so? How are you so sure?"

"I just am."

The others returned, Wendy served toast and Bette did a second round of hot buttered rum, then a third. Soon they were laughing bawdily, joyously, as they recalled stories from childhood. Anne fit in easily with the siblings, graciously entertained by their stories.

The girls came downstairs.

Emma and Dawn asked if they could take Mimi ice-skating on the pond, and Jack said, "We'll have to drill down to check that it's frozen solid first. Care to join, Henry?"

The pond was on land that no longer belonged to the Shaws, but the new landowners had generously said the Shaws and other neighbors were free to fish in it, swim in it, skate on it, picnic by it; whatever they pleased.

On the walk, Henry marveled at all the development and changes to the land as they passed through. He pointed at a house along the way. "Was that the bungalow?" he asked Jack, incredulous.

Jack nodded. Back when they were children, a renovation and

addition to the bungalow had changed the design of that house and doubled its size. In the years since, there had been another addition to the house, and then the family who owned it subdivided the property so that in-laws could build nearby. Then a garage went up. Then another subdivision and a third house. At some point, the new builds had required the owner to cut down the towering maples that had once surrounded and provided shade to the bungalow.

Jack nodded at the old bungalow and said, "There are kids there who Emma and Dawn play with sometimes."

Emma added, "Yes. And a grandpa who smells of pee."

Henry swept his hand broadly out all around him and said to his nieces and daughter, "Did you girls know that all this land used to be—"

Emma interrupted, rolling her eyes, "*Yes*, we know it all used to be fields that belonged to Grandpa Shaw. Blah, blah, blah. Who cares?"

Back at the house, the women chatted in the kitchen until Sam and Rose and their twins, Jess and Pammie, arrived a few hours later.

Sam's twins instantly filled the home with chaos: a wild game involving a large lightweight ball on a string, a quick flare-up, and then they united with near hysteria over the pies cooling on their racks.

"When can we have a piece?" Jess demanded of his mother, jabbing a finger very close to the pie's steaming center.

Rose said, "That's up to our hostesses."

The pies had been planned for after dinner, but Wendy said, "We'll cut into one of them as soon as it's cooled down."

"Fine! Fine! Fine!" Jess stamped his small foot and tore into another room with his sister.

Sam apologized to his sisters for the behavior of his children, though neither he nor Rose made any real effort to settle them.

Rose said, "It's so nice of you to host us. What can I do to help with dinner?"

Bette said, "We're all set, let's go ahead and show you to a room and get you settled."

Sam said, "Who are we missing?"

"Jack, Henry, and the girls are out ice-skating," Wendy said. "So I guess the only one we're still waiting on is Maeve."

"Is she bringing anyone?"

"I don't know," Wendy said. "She said she might have a guest but didn't go into detail. I don't know when she's getting in either, just that she's coming."

At dinnertime, they added two card tables to the dining room table to accommodate everyone. They set places for Maeve and a guest. Wendy and Bette served beef and sweet potatoes and beans, and dessert. Jack was seated next to Maeve's empty place and he commented on how much she would have enjoyed the pies. After eating and cleaning up, a small group settled in at the piano, where Jack plunked away at chords and sang carols, and others played charades. They drank red wine and ate pfeffernuesse by the fire and turned on the television, where *We're No Angels* was airing.

All but Wendy and Sam had retired to bed by the time the movie ended.

Wendy poured the last of the bottle of red into Sam's glass. "How are things at the cannery?"

"Rose's dad's looking to retire completely within the year so I've been taking on more. It's boring stuff. Fish in cans. How's Jack been?"

"Really good, as far as I can tell," Wendy said. "Couple years sober. Does well at work. He's great with the kids. He was close with Thomas before the whole fiasco with the commune, and Bette's girls just adore him."

"That's good. That's good." Sam tipped back his wine to finish it in one swallow. He cracked his knuckles, exhaled, looked at his sister, then at the fire, then back at her, his eyes dark and piercing. "Wendy, I've been wanting to tell you something for a long time," he finally said stiffly. "I thought it would be better face-to-face . . . About the day Mom died. You found her body and called me into the room to wait there while you went to get Dad."

"Yes."

"There was a note," Sam said. "I approached her for a closer look and glanced at the bedside table while you were gone. She had written a suicide note on that pad. I ripped it out. I took it."

"I know," Wendy said.

Sam's head snapped up. "What?"

"I approached the body to make sure she was gone, before I came to get you. I looked at the notepad and started to read the note; I'd already taught myself to read by that time. I hadn't told anyone."

"What! But I had no idea. So you—wait . . . But . . ." Sam felt paralyzed as this knowledge took hold. He could hardly grasp it yet. Everything was changed! "What . . . ?" His thoughts banged around. Could he possibly be this close to having an answer, or even a truth? "What did the note say?" he heaved. "What do you remember? What exactly did she say?"

"I was still just learning to read," Wendy said, "so I was very slow, and her handwriting, you remember, it was so hard to read, especially those later years. So I didn't read the whole thing. Didn't get very far at all. But what I did read, what she said . . ." Wendy's gaze was so faraway it was like her eyes were on another galaxy. "It changed the way I thought about . . . It *reached* me," she said. Then she turned sharply to her brother. "Wait. You *didn't* read it? I thought you just said—"

"I put the note in the fire because it made me so mad, so no, I didn't read beyond . . . So no, I've never stopped thinking, wondering, thinking—Wendy—what did she say?" Sam was frantic, so close to recovering the lost words, the haunted ones, that he was gasping for air and fighting the urge to take his sister by her shoulders and shake loose the truth from within her just to get to it faster. "The part that changed you . . . or the way you thought about . . . What were those words?"

Wendy said, "She said that she loved us."

"I saw that much," Sam said, adrenaline slamming behind his eyes, so greedy for more. He was rotating both hands impatiently in the air between them. "I read that far. What else? What else?"

"But that was as far as I got," Wendy said.

"No," Sam said, "no, there had to be more. Because, see, I read the beginning, too, and it made me so mad I couldn't even bring myself to . . . So there had to be more. The part that *reached* you, like you said. What was *that* part?"

"That was as far as I got."

"But . . ." Sam slumped forward, his insides pitching back and forth in a confusing state of ruin. "Just that she loved us? That meant nothing! Remember how we used to talk about her? Remember how we felt? We hated her, Wen. You did, too. How could those words, *so little*, have possibly have meant anything to you?"

"They didn't feel little to me. And it wasn't only that she said she loved us," Wendy spoke carefully, "but also, it made me think about . . . her handwriting, for example. How shaky with the pen. How difficult, I realized, it must have been for her to write a full page and how long it must have taken her. It had been years since she'd written more than three or four words at a time. And how brave it was of her to write a note at all. Knowing how we felt about her."

"But . . ." Sam was still struggling to grasp the full trajectory of events. "If it meant so much to you, why didn't you say something when you realized I took it? Didn't you want everyone else to see it and be changed by it, to feel the way you did?"

"Not necessarily. I wasn't convinced that it was easier to feel what I was feeling."

"What do you mean?"

"Part of me felt like it would be easier to just keep the armor up. Easier to let go of someone who left without even saying good-bye to us."

Sam was reeling.

"I left the room knowing you would read the note and make a decision about whether or not to share it. I *wanted* you to," Wendy explained. "I wanted someone else to be in charge and take care of things for once, and I thought you were the best one."

"And when you started talking like it was probably an accident?" Sam said.

"I thought I was following your lead. I thought that was what *you* thought was best, since you had done away with the proof."

"I didn't know what I was doing," Sam insisted. "I was wrong. And then . . . I thought *I* was following *your* lead, saying it might have been an overdose. I can't believe this. Wendy, what did we do?"

"We were kids," Wendy said. "We were just kids."

"Think about what was lost!" Sam said, confused and still grappling to accept the cruelty of this. He didn't understand how Wendy was so calm about it. "That whole page."

"Whatever else she wrote," Wendy said, "I imagine she started with the most important thing. Don't you think?"

"But we'll never *know*," he said. "I regret it every single day."

Wendy said with genuine surprise, "I hope you don't."

"I do," Sam said. "How did you get over it? How did you let go of those words?"

"Sam," Wendy said, "I barely even think about that letter anymore. Honest to God. I had no idea you've been suffering like this. We were just kids. Why did you never tell me how you were suffering? If I knew . . ."

Sam rocked back and forth. "We lost so much," he said, not exactly sure what he was referring to; it was all so muddled.

Then he realized, of course, he meant a mother. The lost words were something but not everything, and maybe not even all that important; like Norma from the cannery had once said, words were just words, even the final ones. But the loss of a mother, well that was so much, whether she was a good one or a bad one, a healthy or sick one, an easy or hard one. And whether her love for you was made known every day, or was as strange and impossible as a miracle; one that either reached you and touched you, or didn't. One that you either believed in, in spite of everything, or you couldn't.

It was quiet for a long while.

Eventually Wendy asked, "What are you thinking now?"

"Jack," Sam said with difficulty. "He always knew it was suicide. He never believed us about it being a mistake, and he was always so angry about there not being a note. He never got over that. If I tell him now, he'll hate me for the lie. But I feel like we owe it to him and the others."

Wendy sighed. Her chest felt squished on the inside. Jack did hate secrets and lies more than anything. And though he had mellowed considerably in the past few years, he was still quick to anger.

"What should I do?" Sam said. "Should I tell everyone? I'll do whatever you think I should do. I never know what to do."

Wendy didn't like this responsibility, she didn't want it.

She had made her peace with the secret of the note so long ago, grateful that Sam had made the decision to get rid of it. She had not carried guilt. They were kids, faced with an unthinkable, impossible moment, and even if she would choose something different now, she hadn't allowed herself to be tormented about it. How much would it change for her siblings, she wondered, now all grown, to have the suicide confirmed and to learn of their mother's love for them, expressed in her final moments? Would it change anything for anyone else? It would undoubtedly complicate things between them now; Sam was right that the others, especially Jack, would feel terribly betrayed by the secret he and Wendy had kept. Was the truth worth the rift it would almost certainly create?

Emotions rippled and rushed through her in a sequence that did not make sense.

Sam rose for a glass of water and Wendy could see he wasn't going to go to bed, or let this drop, until she'd given her opinion.

As Wendy thought more, a decision eventually reached her, as decisions nearly always did: solid as a brick. Sam was right; the others deserved to know. They were kids then, but now they were not, and it was wrong to keep this information from their siblings any longer. Jack had always maintained that it was suicide. He deserved to have this confirmed. And they all deserved to know that their mother had had the desire, and found the courage, to say goodbye.

Wendy thought more.

Finally, she said, "I'm going to tell Jack."

Sam looked at her.

She said, "I'll tell him that we found a note, the words we read and how much we didn't read, and that we've kept all of this secret all this time."

"I can't let you take this on," Sam said. "It was my decision back then to destroy the note. If we're going to tell, I've got to be the one to do it."

Wendy was shaking her head. "No," she said. "It will be me. Jack and I have been living together for years now. It will be better coming from me."

"This isn't why I brought it up, Wendy. I wanted you to tell me what to do, not do it yourself."

Wendy drummed the tabletop with her fingers. She was sure now, so she felt better, and it was time for bed. "I'll wait till the holiday's over and everybody's gone so it's not a scene and doesn't spoil anybody's time, but then I'll tell him. And I'll tell the others, too."

A week later, after they had cleaned up from the Christmas guests and were still enjoying leftovers and the afterglow of the holiday and time together, Wendy would go outside to join Jack in the afternoon as he was shoveling snow from the driveway. She would watch him for a few moments, noticing how radiant his cheeks had become with the cold and the effort, and how much he looked like their father, before approaching.

They would stand in the middle of the swirling wind, and she would tell him about the note; confirmation of their mother's suicide, the words she opened with, the words that followed but had been lost and remained unknown. Wendy would convey that she and Sam were sorry for keeping the suicide a secret, a mystery, all these years. Jack would listen and then fall silent for a very long time, looking into the distance, though in the heavy snow it was impossible to see much, or far. Wendy would try to follow his eyes, and they would go nowhere.

Finally, Jack would say quietly, "But I . . ." and then he would trail off.

What words were meant to follow? Wendy's mind ticked

through the possibilities: *But I already knew . . .* Or, *But I thought you said . . .* Or, *But I believed you . . .* Or, *But I would have had such a different life . . .* She would not get her answer, though; it would seem Jack had said everything he wanted to say on the matter, because a moment later, he would be back to shoveling.

Wendy would wish that she could open her brother's mind like a piece of fruit to examine every bruise and sweetness so that it was all plain and intelligible to her. But of course the mind was nothing like fruit; the mind was a pearl drawn from the depths of the ocean, wild and rare and totally mysterious even to the creature in whom it lived.

Wendy would tell the other siblings about the note over the course of the next few days, Bette and Lane in person and the rest of them over the phone. Then she would report to Sam that it had been taken care of.

On Christmas Eve morning, they had established a plan for sledding over at the hill behind the Baptist church. There were not enough sleds to go around for all the children, so Wendy sent them with some baking sheets, too. She and her sisters stayed at the house and worked on braided pastries. Jack stayed behind, too, in case Maeve arrived. He was so eager and didn't want to miss even a few minutes with her.

When the sledding crew returned a few hours later, Jess had rusty flakes around his nostrils. "I got a bloody nose and made red in the snow and there was so much it almost made Emma faint," he reported.

Some of the children went back outside for a snowball fight and others stayed in to play crazy eights. Lane slipped away for a nap. Jack asked Wendy again about when Maeve was supposed to arrive and Wendy said again that she didn't know; Maeve had never specified, and hadn't been in touch in a few days.

A neighbor came with a little white box of fresh peanut brittle, and Wendy insisted she stay for cookies and tea or a toddy. The children watched and scowled as the neighbor ate the cookies Wendy offered, some of which the children had decorated with intention, and for themselves.

They all got cleaned up and sat for dinner at five. They once again set a place for Maeve and her guest. Jack proposed a toast even though he was drinking water and the family was not much for grandiose gestures, even at the holidays, and the rest of them said, *Sure, sure, if you must.*

They passed prime rib and corn and stewed apples and red wine and ales around and around the table, then Wendy brought out an assortment of shortbread and pastries and cheese and jams and fruit butters and candied nuts. Before the dessert platter had made it around the table, the front door flew open without a knock and a red-faced Maeve entered with a gust of wind, singing, "Ho-ho-ho!"

"Yay!" her nieces and nephew cried.

Jack rose to help with her bags.

Wendy pointed out the place settings for Maeve and her

absent guest, in between Jack and Sam, and she made Maeve a plate of the main course.

Maeve said, "I broke up with my boyfriend last night, sorry I forgot to tell you not to bother with an extra setting."

Emma was sitting across from Maeve and her eyes snapped wide open. "You broke up with your boyfriend?"

"That's what boyfriends are for, isn't it?" Maeve said.

"It is?" Emma looked at her aunt in wonder.

At the far end of the table, the twins were making moves to use pear butter as face paint, and Rose intervened. Lane got up to put on a new record, *Christmas with Patti Page*, and when Jack sang along loudly in his falsetto, Maeve joined with operatic flair.

Emma said, "Auntie Maeve, did you bring us presents? I didn't see any when you came in."

"I did not," Maeve said. "But I heard a rumor that Santa might have."

The adults had conferred on gifts weeks earlier. Since Dawn and the twins were still all-in for Santa, the adults had decided to stash gifts in cars or the attic until late Christmas Eve night, when they would bring them in to fill the space under the tree.

They sent the dessert platter around the table another time, and Bette brought out port and scotch. They drank and sang and laughed. Eventually and in stages, everyone made their way from the table to the living room to stretch out on couches, or to the kitchen to help with cleanup. *The Bishop's Wife* was playing on the television. Jack added logs to the fire, and it flared high. A second bottle of scotch was opened, but little was consumed. Yawns and murmurs about the bigness and tastiness of the meal and the goodness of the day. Idle complaints about the movie. Fresh snowfall bulging at the windowsills. Before the end of the movie, the twins, Dawn, Emma, and Mimi had all fallen asleep and needed to be coaxed up to bed by their parents. Once the children were gone, the grown-ups gathered presents and arranged them beneath the tree. Wendy made a note from Santa thanking the children for the cookies. Soon everyone had retired to bed except for Jack and Maeve.

Maeve said, "Care to join me for a snowy walk? I'm dying for a cigarette and some fresh air."

The two of them bundled up. A gust of wind met them as soon as they stepped outside, and Jack felt the cold like pain in the inside of his nose. They fumbled to light their cigarettes on the porch, then trudged out the driveway. They had to speak loudly to hear each other over surges of wind.

Jack said, "How long can you stay?"

"I've gotta head back first thing, day after tomorrow," Maeve said. "I'll stay for Christmas dinner and the night but probably be up and out before anyone else is awake on the twenty-sixth."

"So soon? Why? Didn't your practice close down for the full week?"

"Yeah, but . . ." Maeve took a drag on her cigarette. "You know how it is. Things to do. Gotta keep it moving."

"Okay," Jack said, and he said, *Okay, okay*, inside his head a few more times to keep from feeling much more about this—like bitterness or resentment or personal injury—because any of these, he knew, could so easily ignite something worse in him. *It's okay*, he told himself. And it was.

"How are you doing?" Maeve said. "Do you hear anything from Camille?"

"Once or twice a year, just a hello," Jack said. "She's remarried, two kids now. Still up in Minnesota. She's good. It's good. I'm better, I think, with other people's kids than I would be with my own. Better with other people's lives in general."

"How do you mean?"

"I have better instincts, and more capacity for goodness, when it comes to everyone outside of myself."

"I see." Maeve's cigarette had gone out so they paused their walking so she could relight it. "Bette's girls seem like a handful."

"They are."

"How's Lane doing with all this business with Thomas and all? Is he still off singing 'Kumbaya' with a bunch of losers in the woods?"

Jack nodded. He thought back to his conversation with Lane on the way home from Tennessee.

He remembered many conversations with Maeve over the years, in which Maeve had tried to get him to calm down about John Winthrop, tried to convince him that what he was suggesting could not be true; that Lane could not have stayed with a man who had violated her. But Maeve, with her fancy psychology degree, had been wrong, and Jack had been right, his long-standing anger at John Winthrop fully vindicated. And perhaps some other things about himself, Jack thought hopefully, could be accounted for by this, too—not just his long-standing anger at John Winthrop, but his long-standing anger at the world, his tortured relation to his place in it. He had the urge to tell Maeve all of this but stopped short, deciding that the mysteries of Lane's teenage years, and her marriage, and her life in Chesterfield, had never been Jack's nor anyone else's to speculate about nor to malign. It was always up to Lane, of course, not her siblings, how she wanted to deal with it and what sort of protection, if any, she wanted or needed from the truth. But on the other hand, Jack countered himself, hadn't he, too, suffered on account of it? So didn't he, too, then, deserve to look this story square in the eye, to wrestle it down into something he could manage, and harness for his own purposes? Didn't he deserve to show it and tell it and make it known, make it part of his story, too? No, he thought, God no, of course he didn't deserve this.

Jack tipped his head backward to clear his mind, and was surprised that even through the snow, he could see many stars. Some bright, some blue, some faded, some that seemed to pulse with life, and then there were all the ones he could not see but knew were out there, too; the black holes, and also all the ones not yet winked into existence.

He had stopped walking, and Maeve urged him along by linking her elbow through his. "We'll freeze to death," she said.

Soon they reached a small brick ranch house set back off the road, with colored bulbs strung across the front overhang, and a warm golden light pooling from the main room. Jack thought he could faintly hear laughter from inside, then thought, no, it must be his imagination, the sound couldn't possibly travel this far.

"That's a new house, isn't it?" Maeve said. Like nearly everything in sight, it sat on property that used to belong to the Shaws.

"It's been there a couple years, actually," Jack said.

Maeve read the name on the mailbox aloud. "The Gearings," she said. "What are they like? What's their story?"

Jack gazed at the house. Woodsmoke huffed out meekly from the chimney. He could see several bobbing heads through the windows and perhaps a blinking television set, but all of this was obscured by the warm golden light that poured forth, the whole house ablaze with it, so vivid and acute it seemed to actually reach out with fingers to illuminate something inside Jack.

"What's their story?" Maeve asked again.

"I've never met them, but Wendy has and she says they're nice," Jack said, at a full stop once again, marveling at this luminescence.

Maeve pulled at Jack's arm, saying, "Come on," and he obeyed and on they went.

Their cigarettes were long gone and the wind was picking up and Jack didn't know how much farther Maeve intended to go before turning back for home, but he was willing to endure a few more minutes of this cold if it made her happy.

Jack wondered if another Christmas would ever be held at the

Shaw family house and if so, if Maeve would come for a longer stay. He wasn't angry that she had been so late in arriving, without a good excuse, and would leave already the day after tomorrow, probably before anyone else was even awake. Not angry. Just wondering what accounted for the difference between the ones who couldn't stand to stay and the ones who couldn't stand to leave.

Wendy's words about the neighbors in the little brick ranch house returned to Jack's mind: *Nice family.* That was it, that was all Wendy had to say on the matter of the Gearing family.

It occurred to Jack that the Gearings and other neighbors likely said the same about the Shaw family when passing by their home. *Nice family*, the neighbors might say, or maybe, *Not so nice*, and either way, that would be it, end of the conversation, end of the story of the Shaws as far as anyone outside their family was concerned.

And who could blame them, Jack thought. They all had their own homes to return to, their own families to care for and contend with, their own set of stories to negotiate, to tell or not tell, to remember or forget, to honor or to dispense with, their own private collections of darkness and light, truths and lies. Our little hearts can carry only so much in one lifetime, after all. And even just one family, God help us, even just one, Jack thought, is so much, it is so much.

Acknowledgments

Immense gratitude to Michelle Tessler, Jack Shoemaker, Megan Fishmann, Yukiko Tominaga, Nicole Caputo, Wah-Ming Chang, Laura Berry, Rachel Fershleiser, Jennifer Alton, Chandra Wohleber, Jordan Koluch, Alyson Forbes, Dan López, and to my family, my truest joy and guiding light.

© Rachel Herr

REBECCA KAUFFMAN received her MFA in creative writing from New York University. She is the author of *Another Place You've Never Been*, which was long-listed for the Center for Fiction First Novel Prize; *The Gunners*, which received the Premio Tribùk dei Librai; and *The House on Fripp Island*. Originally from rural northeastern Ohio, Kauffman now lives in Virginia. Find out more at rebeccakauffman.net.